Life After Death

Life After Death

TJ Graham

PRODIGY GOLD BOOKS

PHILADELPHIA * LOS ANGELES

PRODIGY
GOLDBOOKS

LIFE AFTER DEATH

A Prodigy Gold Book

Prodigy Gold E-book edition/June 2018

Prodigy Gold Paperback edition/June 2018

Copyright (c) 2018 by TJ Graham

Library of Congress Catalog Card Number: On File

Website: http://www.prodigygoldbooks.com

Author's e-mail: tjgrahamwriter@gmail.com

ISBN 978-1-939665-53-9

Published simultaneously in the US and Canada

PRINTED IN THE UNITED STATES OF AMERICA

ACKNOWLEDGEMENTS

Thanks to my friends and family. This list is long and so is their patience.

Kelvin Goodwin, Tonette Earl, Keyonia Parsons, Scarlett King, Jarid Manos, Corrina Martinez, Sultana Sams and for all those who served as my sounding boards and the much-needed encouragement to complete this book. Thank you all for taking this journey with me.

I also want to give a special thank you to Mr. Keith Nelson. We discussed this book over lunch the day that you died. Your motiving words are always with me. You are truly missed. Rest in peace, my friend.

Finally, I would also like to thank Rahiem Brooks, editor of Prodigy Gold Books, for his guidance and taking a chance on me. The best is yet to come.

Life

After

Death

PROLOGUE

Without saying a word, without making a sound, almost without breathing, Dr. Lang sat motionless with his head between his knees. His hands cupped the nape of his neck. For three days, he had not showered, shaved, or slept. He wore the same blue suit—now a wrinkled distortion of its style and cost. And for three days his wife and sixteen-year-old daughter had gone missing.

Three days ago, he had come home late from his office. He saw his wife's black Mercedes parked in the garage and expected that she would be ready to continue the argument they'd started the night before. No doubt, their daughter was in her room, glued to her cell phone, oblivious to anything else going on in the house.

Instead, he found no one. Nothing left indicating where they might have been. None of his phone calls or text messages were returned. There were no signs of forced entry or a struggle. No note signed: Goodbye. No witness to their departure. No friend or family member aware of their whereabouts.

Silence.

He immediately called the Memphis Police Department only to be informed by an indifferent officer that he had to wait twenty-four hours before filing a missing person's report.

That was three days ago.

The police had interviewed him. The report was filed. Yet, the two people that he loved the most in the world remained missing. He tried not to let his imagination succumb to the horrors that could have befallen them by now. Burning fear that he would catch a breaking news report leading off with: Two Bodies Found. Now he sat in the police station lobby after confronting the detective who never returned his phone calls. His anger swelled within, drowning out incessant ringing telephones and the tantrum of a toddler sitting on an old woman's lap across from him. Surely, the police knew something by now.

Anything.

He was dismissed with the standard police lines: *"We're doing the best we can. We feel for you. We'll call you as soon as anything comes up."* In the end, they had no idea what had happened to his family. Andre wasn't convinced that they even cared.

He leaned back against the dingy cinderblock wall, caressing his gold wedding band. He rose to his feet and reluctantly took the somber drive home. Outside, he hardly noticed the crisp November air stinging his face.

Thanksgiving is in three days, he thought, maneuvering his silver Range Rover into traffic. He lamented his decision to argue with Rene over her desire to spend the holiday in Raleigh with her family. She looked forward to it, but he preferred lounging around Memphis watching football games and eating leftovers. He shook his head in disgust. *What a stupid argument.* He was being so selfish when all his wife wanted was to spend time with her family. She rarely saw them. Tears trickled down his face as he slammed his fist against the dashboard. He wanted to scream. *Why was this happening to them? Why couldn't things be normal?*

Andre pulled into his driveway terrified of the tormenting silence, he knew awaited. Somehow, he found the courage to make it to the front door. It was ajar. Rene's bronze heart keychain dangled in the lock. His heart jackhammered inside his chest.

"Rene. Zhuri," he yelled, flinging the door wide open. The nightmare was finally over.

"Rene. Zhuri."

He ran from room to room. *Upstairs. They must be upstairs.* He flew up the staircase, his feet barely touching a step leading to their bedroom.

He couldn't believe it. They were safely in his bed. Covered by the floral comforter. Liquid relief poured from his eyes.

"Rene, baby. Where have you been?" He stroked the larger of the two silhouettes.

No response.

"Rene?...Zhuri?"

Andre felt his knees weaken, threatening to collapse beneath him. His hands trembled. The ominous feeling that he had been trying to ignore engulfed his spirit as he slowly pulled back the cover.

"Oh, God...Please, God, nooo."

Andre dropped to his knees. Lying in the bed, their vacant eyes fixed on him, was Rene, the love of his life, and his sweet, innocent daughter Zhuri. Dead. Blood seeping from their mutilated stomachs. He struggled to make sense of the horror scene before him. Finding no rationale, realizing that this was no nightmare that he could escape, he held his head back to let out a soul shattering scream. The two lights in his life. His reasons for living. Gone. Forever.

CHAPTER 1

Atlanta, Georgia
Three years Later

Daybreak. Traces of the golden September sun crept pass Mackenzie's partially closed draperies, bathing her room in an amber glow. On cue, her alarm clock screamed that it was six a.m. A new workweek was beginning whether she liked it or not.

Mackenzie stirred beneath her warm duvet, ignoring the clock's orders to start her morning routine. After a minute or two of its persistence she slowly rose, recalling the surreal events of the previous night: flashing cameras, generous applause, and an endless flow of champagne. Her colleagues honored her with an Associated Press Award for Investigative Journalism. Her first. Not quite the coveted Pulitzer Prize that she had set her goals on, but it was nice to be recognized for her hard work.

She hit the clock in the precise spot to silence it, then pulled the duvet back over her head. *Hell,* she thought, a sly smile on her face. *No one would mind if I called out today. I'm an award- winning journalist, right?* She chuckled at her newfound arrogance.

"Damn." She groaned, remembering her responsibilities like a looming deadline, and the major press conference she had been assigned to cover for the paper today. "I need to get my ass to the office."

The house phone rang. Mackenzie squinted at the caller ID. It was her mother. Feeling a little guilty, she tucked her head beneath a pillow and let the call go to voicemail. Her mother probably called to congratulate her on the achievement. No doubt, she would slip day-ruining hints about companionship being just as important as career ambitions into the conversation. She meant well, but Mrs. Gwendolyn Mae Jones, could not seem to understand that a woman could be fulfilled raising her children alone. Even if that woman were widowed.

Her cell phone rang a moment later. Mackenzie sprang to life when she saw that it was her best friend, Joel. She put him on speaker then sat up against the headboard.

"Mornin', boo. Did you have fun last night?" she asked, wondering if he remembered how drunk he had gotten at the reception. Or how he had blatantly flirted with her editor's twenty-five-year-old son.

"Mornin', Z," he said. He moaned from a slight hangover. "Everything is kind of fuzzy, but I at least remember jumping up when they called your name."

"Maybe that's for the best, 'cause you were kind of wild."

"Not too wild I hope?" he asked with a hint of concern in his voice.

"Um, I think I'll plead the fifth."

"That bad, huh? Knowing your petty ass, an embarrassing video clip will pop on Instagram or something."

"True. Get me those Jimmy Choo's I tried on at Neiman's last week, and you'll have nothing to worry about."

"Blackmail is so beneath you."

"Not when it comes to cute shoes." She chuckled. "You're up early."

"Uh, don't remind me," Joel said. "I have a very early meeting with a new client. Plus, I just wanted to tell you again how proud I am of you. You've worked really hard for this and you've overcome a lot."

"Awww, thank you, Joel. You love me, don't you?"

"See. You took it too far. You know I just keep you around to attract men."

They both laughed, fully aware of how much they meant to each other. They had meet in a freshman English class at Clark Atlanta University. After spending the entire semester secretly crushing on him, throwing ignored hints, Mackenzie asked Joel to the school's annual homecoming ball. He stunned her when he said: "OK, cool. But, you know, I'm gay, right? When are we going shopping for our outfits?"

Since then, they had developed into best friends. "Are you going to work today?"

"I'm going to have to take an entire bottle of Advil, but yeah, I'm going in. I have an article to finish up and a press conference to cover at three."

"By cover, you mean get a front row seat to be nosey."

"You know it. It got my name etched on this damn piece of glass, didn't it?" She admired the glass, pentagon shaped award, she had placed on her nightstand.

He yawned. "Good point. I'll call you later. I need to get ready for my meeting. Plus, I know you need to get your brats ready for school. Let's meet for lunch or something."

"OK. Let's try that Thai restaurant that everyone at work is always talking about. The Spice Pot, I think. Your treat of course."

"Wow. This award must really be going to your head. Now, you're a blackmailer *and* a freeloader." He hung up more than happy to pay.

Mackenzie glided her hand along the right side of the bed. She glanced at a picture of her husband on the nightstand next to her award, admiring his cappuccino-tone skin and hazel eyes. Suddenly, her accomplishment seemed trivial, her bed colder and emptier than before.

"Good morning, Marlon," she whispered. The tears in her eyes dried up when her six-year-old identical twin sons, Rashad and Antwan, burst into the room. They wore their favorite Black Panther pajamas.

"Congratulations, mom!" they shouted in unison, jumping into bed with her.

Mackenzie kissed their honey-brown cheeks. "Thank you, babies." She smiled, tousling their curly manes.

Her fifteen-year-old daughter, Traci, came in behind them, carrying a tray of food. She was dressed earlier than usual for school.

"Good morning, mom," she sang with a kiss to Mackenzie's cheek. "I'm so proud of you." She placed the tray of waffles topped with strawberries, scrambled eggs, and chicken sausage links across Mackenzie's lap.

"Thank you, Sweet T," she said, calling her by the nickname her dad had given her. When Traci was a toddler she would always sneak sweets. "You didn't have to do all of this."

Traci sat on the edge of the bed. She shrugged in that nonchalant teenager way.

"No big deal. You do a million times more for us. Besides, I was up already. Remember, I asked you to let me take an Uber to school to finish up my biology experiment for the science club. Competition submissions are due next week."

"Oh, yeah, I forgot. Sorry, baby," Mackenzie said. She took a bite of sausage while the twins helped themselves to her waffle.

"It's Okay." Traci said, looking down at her cell phone.

Mackenzie couldn't be prouder of her daughter. She looked cute in her blue and green pleated skirt and blue blazer over a white Oxford. It was hard to believe that she was going on sixteen. She was already five-six with thick black hair, hazel eyes, and defined features like her father. Traci had also inherited Marlon's keen mind and his fascination with science.

"What's your experiment about again?"

Traci's phone chimed. She jumped up. "I'll explain it to you later. Love you, mom." She gave Mackenzie another peck on the cheek before hurrying down the stairs and out the kitchen door.

Mackenzie looked at the clock. *I'd better get moving myself.*

"Okay boys are you excited about your field trip to the aquarium today?" she asked the twins.

"Yeah," they shouted in harmony, syrup dripping from Antwan's chin.

She smiled, reinvigorated by life, and how much she loved her children.

Anxiously, Andre walked through the front door of his new practice. He paused, admiring the meticulous waiting area. Everything was in order. Tawny leather reception chairs. Whimsical artwork on the walls. Magazines were fanned across a dark-stained coffee table. A forty-two-inch TV hung next to a coffee maker prepared to percolate with its first batch of gourmet brew for his patients. It was an office filled with warmth.

It had taken him three years to get to this point. Three years of mourning. Three years of therapy. Three years of prayers. His therapist had told him that his willingness to reestablish his medical practice signified that he was ready to move forward with his life. Most days his heart told him differently.

Andre had moved to Atlanta two years ago. He took an administrative position at Grady Memorial Hospital, helping to ensure that Atlanta's indigent women received quality prenatal care. A noble job. Much different from the affluent women he had as patients in Memphis. They mostly sought his services for discreet abortions.

This time, he planned to have a well-rounded OB/GYN practice, referring patients who sought non-life-threatening abortions to colleagues. Operating this way, he was going against his late wife's beliefs. Dr. Rene Lang, professor of African History at the University of Memphis, was adamantly pro-choice. He could picture her shouting at the pro-lifers who sometimes picketed outside his office building: "A woman has every right to choose what to do with her own body." She would be disappointed to know that he would turn away women who had opted to have an abortion. Even if his work may have cost her and their daughter their lives. Knowing this, he still couldn't help himself.

The medical examiner had determined that the official cause of the death of his wife and daughter had been suffocation. The way their bodies were mutilated lead the Memphis PD to speculate that their murders were the work of an anti-abortion extremist. That theory was never proven, but it devastated him to think that his career contributed in any way.

He walked to the back of the suite to his private office, where the decorative theme was continued. He sat in a comfortable black leather chair behind his desk. It was 6:46 a.m. His new office manager, Paula, arrived daily around 7:00. The first of his new patients was scheduled an hour later. He was confident that he would earn their trust and he would grow his practice, allowing him to settle into a welcomed routine that kept him too busy to feel.

"Dr. Lang?" Paula said, coming through the front door.

"I'm back in my office, Paula," he yelled. "I'll come up in a second." He inhaled, filling his lungs to capacity, then slowly exhaled. "Here we go."

———————

Monday mornings were getting hard for Atlanta sex crimes detective, Keith Wilson. The sense of duty he felt to help people through law enforcement was fading. Lately, he had to force himself to work after spending his weekends trying to cleanse his mind and soul of the evil that people can do to one another.

This Monday was the exception. Unable to sleep, Keith had been up since the predawn hours, laying on his back in his Zen decorated living room. He reviewed the file of the young victim of an infamous rape/murder case. The district attorney had called a press conference to announce that the accused, Thomas Walters, was finally in custody after almost three years of evading capture. Keith was eager to deliver justice to the victim and her family.

He continued to intensely gaze at the photos of the victim—a thirteen-year old girl whose family had sent her to the Walters' Family Annual Summer Camp. Instead of some new experiences and clean fun, she was raped, and her skull bashed in by a wealthy real estate heir to silence her.

Keith put aside her photos. He reached for those of victims in other cases he was currently investigating.

A Hispanic mother of three had been gang raped, robbed, and shot to death.

A hapless seven-year-old deaf boy killed on his way to school. He had dreamed of becoming an astronaut. Instead of exploring the stars, he was sodomized, strangled, and dumped in the woods.

Keith had seen too many files of people who constantly haunted his dreams. People who depended on him to avenge their murders. Keith did not want to fail them. The problem was, he did not know if he could continue as their champion. Somewhere along his fifteen-year career his heart had grown weary. He dreaded the many times he had to visit a parent to tell them the horrible fate of their child, or a spouse because their loved one was not coming home.

Contrary to his easygoing demeanor, Keith was becoming a cynical man. Death was his constant companion, shaping his view of the world as a cruel place where it's icy grip was the only certainty. Recently, Keith had sought out the soul-calming philosophies of Buddhism. He did not officially call himself a Buddhist, but he credited the religion's practice of meditation and spiritual enlightenment with keeping him sane.

The phone rang. Keith reached for it knowing that it was his partner, Leroy Parnell. The young rookie had transferred from the Cleveland PD. He had only been with the APD for about two years, but he was making a name for himself in the sex crimes unit as a quick-witted investigator. An easy friendship had developed between them. Keith found himself confiding in Parnell. His optimistic outlook on life was what Keith needed.

"Yeah," Keith answered, clearing his throat.

"What up, brother?" Parnell said. "Ready for the press conference?"

"Yeah, man. It's a big day for Kendra Stewart's family. They can finally start getting some closure, knowing that that asshole has finally been caught and will be brought to justice."

"Amen to that," Parnell said. "But do you honestly think a jury will find him guilty? I mean a white man with the kind of money that his family throws, accused of killing a poor black girl."

"I honestly don't know, Parnell. I've seen it go either way." Keith glanced at a picture of Kendra. Her lifeless eyes cut into him, crying out for help. Keith squeezed his own eyes shut, hoping to block her out. It didn't work. "But, I just don't see how he can be found innocent. I mean, we've got credible witnesses, collected iron clad evidence, and the fact that he fled the country for three years should be proof enough for anyone."

"Yeah. Proof enough to convict you, me, and most of the world. Not a rich heir with access to high dollar lawyers."

"No. I'm not going to even think like that. I've got a good feeling that asshole is going to get what's coming to him. Karma is a motherfucker," Keith replied, surprised that he wasn't the cynic this time. "I'll talk to you later, Parnell. I'm about to go for a run and then meditate."

"Cool. Maybe a good run and some of that Buddhist stuff will help clear your mind."

I hope so, Keith thought, hanging up.

CHAPTER 2

In silence, fifteen-year-old, Traci Nicole Hill, lay nude in her boyfriend's bed. Staring at the wall posters of Kobe Bryant and Lebron James until they blurred together. After months of being hesitant, she had lost her virginity. Traci had enjoyed the intimacy but wasn't prepared for the emotional confusion that followed. She looked over at Antonio, who was sound asleep. A queasy feeling churned in her stomach.

Guilt.

Guilt from lying to her mother this morning. She skipped school and had sex without a condom. *No condom,* she gasped. Reality chocked her like thick smog. Suddenly, those cheesy public service announcements from TV, preaching the merits of abstinence, or safe sex made a lot of sense.

What had she done? She knew better. She had always been an honor student with a passion for science, sparked early on by her dad. If he were alive, he would be disappointed in her.

Antonio stirred in his sleep. He pulled her closer to him and kissed the back of her neck.

"You OK, bae?"

"Yeah," she whispered timidly.

She had known, Antonio Osborne, since the fifth grade. She knew that he wasn't a virgin, but his constant assurance convinced Traci that she was the one for him. He had even told her that he loved her proving that feeling with sincere actions. Traci was sure that she loved him, too. Being in his strong, athletic arms was where she was meant to be.

The grand clock in the atrium of the Georgia TransWorld building, a 52-story edifice of glass and granite in downtown Atlanta, showed that it was 8:32 am when Mackenzie came rushing in. She was running late because Antwan had puked all over himself in the car, forcing her to turn around midway to her brother, Nathan's house. She usually dropped them off there on school days since all three of Nate's children attended the same school as the twins. Since Mackenzie had to be at work almost an hour before the twins had to be to school, Nate's wife, Beverly, didn't mind getting them off each morning along with her bunch.

Mackenzie was just in time to catch an elevator that was heading up. Entering, she was surprised to see her usually punctual co-worker, Jackie Smalls. She was standing in the rear trying to clean a red stain from her gray slacks.

Jackie was the type of woman one found attractive when she wasn't icy and defensive. She was about thirty-five, petite, and caramel-colored with delicate features hidden behind too much makeup and a permanent scowl. She kept mostly to herself around the office. She never mentioned any kids or love interest, and her fashionable wardrobe showed that she spent a large chunk of her salary in Atlanta's finer boutiques.

"Well, hello, Mrs. Hill," she said, forming ice with each word. She looked up from her stain. "I suppose that congratulations are in order."

Mackenzie smiled politely at Jackie's insincere praise. "Thank you, Jackie. That means a lot coming from you."

Jackie looked up again. *Here it comes*, Mackenzie predicted.

"But you know, Mackenzie," she said, sounding particularly petty. "I probably shouldn't say anything, but a lot of people are saying that several other journalists deserved that award a lot more than you."

"Oh really, Jackie? Which people?" Mackenzie couldn't care less, but she indulged Jackie's need to validate herself.

"Well, Mackenzie. You know that I am a professional. I never reveal my sources," Jackie smugly replied. "Let's just say that's what's going around."

"Well, Ms. *Smalls* you can tell your sources that I'll remember how much I don't deserve my AP award while I'm picking out my new display case." She turned to face the doors. "You know, the kind that's well lit up to show it off."

Unable to think of a snappy comeback fast enough, Jackie rolled her eyes, and went back to her stain. Mackenzie felt Jackie's eyes burning a hole in the back of her head as they continued the elevator ride in silence.

Mackenzie smiled. *Joel would be proud of the way I handled that*, she thought.

The Atlanta Star was housed on the 36th floor in modern offices that boasted walnut wall paneling, frosted glass office doors, and touches of chrome. Only a few of the journalist who worked at the mid-sized newspaper had their own private offices. After a little over two years of hard work, Mackenzie was glad to be one of them. Her office was small, but it did overlook downtown Atlanta. She liked to gaze out of the window imagining what kind of life stories each passerby could tell her.

She was just about to step into her office when her editor, Robert Montgomery, a grizzly man with round wire rimmed glasses, surprised her from behind.

He shouted, "Congratulations, Mackenzie."

Mackenzie stood, blushing as her coworkers showered her with applause and confetti. She even saw Jackie in the rear forcing herself to clap. The ovation died down when Montgomery begin to speak in his commanding baritone. "Mackenzie," he said. "I would like to congratulate you on a job well done. On behalf of myself and the staff, we would like to present you with a small token of our appreciation for the prestige your work brings to our little paper." He gave her a small rectangular package wrapped in eggshell blue paper. Her co-workers applauded again.

"Speech. Speech," someone yelled out.

Misty eyed, Mackenzie, began speaking, looking out at her coworkers smiling faces. "I came to the Star during an extremely difficult time in my life. I just want to say thank you to everyone for the support and encouragement that you all have given me." She paused as she became overwhelmed with emotion. "I promise to continue to do my best."

More applause and cheers followed.

Montgomery embraced her, as did a few of her coworkers.

"You did real good, Mackenzie," he said, wiping her eyes with his handkerchief. "Now back to work. Don't think you get to slack off just because you have one AP award. That comes with your second or third."

There was weak laughter amongst the staff as they began to disburse. They had upcoming deadlines to meet.

Mackenzie walked into her office. She closed the door and sat at her desk contemplating the last four years of her life. She placed the gift next to a silver framed photo of her husband who had passed away three years earlier. Tears flowed down her face.

"Well," she said, speaking softly to the picture. "Looks like we did it, Marlon. Looks like we made it."

She picked it up, staring at it as if her eyes had the power to magically bring him back to her. Marlon Anthony Hill passed away at thirty-seven, following a battle with lymphoma. His death devastated Mackenzie, plunging her into a reclusion. She quit freelance writing and began financially supporting their children with Marlon's substantial life insurance settlement and their investments. Realizing that she was emotionally neglecting them, she fought her way back to the land of the living; knowing that things would never be the same without her soulmate.

She stroked the picture. It was one she had taken of him at the party she gave to celebrate the doctorate in microbiology that he had earned from Emory University. He looked so handsome. His dark curly hair, his piercing eyes full of pride as he held up his degree. Mackenzie held the picture to her heart.

She and Marlon had met during the spring of their respective junior years on the campus of Emory. Mackenzie was there doing interviews on the political views of black students at predominately white schools for the CAU newspaper. Marlon was one of the first black students that she saw, so she had asked him for an interview. As they talked that sunny afternoon, Marlon charmed her with his social awareness, corny humor, and brilliant mind. They had their first official date a few days later and were together in love from then on until his untimely death took him away.

Mackenzie sat the picture back in its place. She grabbed a tissue from the box on her desk to wipe her eyes.

Stop crying, boo bear, she knew Marlon would say if he saw her that way. *You've got work to do. Stay strong for me. Can't stop now.* Bravely,

Mackenzie brought out the research on her current article, booted up her laptop, and prepared to do what she loved: Write.

———————

Around 11 a.m. Joel texted Mackenzie to see if she was free for lunch. Just after noon, he drove up to meet her across from her building. He had the top down on his candy apple red BMW 4 Series, sported mirrored aviator sunglasses, and blasted Janet Jackson from her *Rhythm Nation* days. He flashed a bright smile when he saw Mackenzie.

"You're not eighteen anymore, boo." She teased him.

Joel squinted at her over the top of his shades. "Well, tell that to my eighteen-year-old appetite cause I'm starving." He chuckled. "Now get your ass in this car."

Joel suggested that they call in a to-go order from the favorite soul food spot from college and eat their lunch in Centennial Olympic Park since the weather was so pleasant.

The Busy Beaver restaurant, located near the Atlanta University Center consortium of HBCUs, was a neighborhood staple. It didn't look like much on the outside, but more than made up for what it lacked in aesthetics with its food. As usual, it was every bit as busy as its name proclaimed, bustling with the familiar crowd of AUC students and staff, mingling with loyal patrons who could never get enough of the tasty soul food. Mackenzie and Joel picked up their orders of fried fish, collard greens, and mac 'n' cheese.

Centennial Olympic Park was full of people taking advantage of the unseasonably warm mid-September day and clear blue skies. They set at a table across from the park's dancing fountains.

Mackenzie told Joel how Mr. Montgomery and her coworkers had surprised her with the gift of a monogramed sterling silver Tiffany pen set and had showered her with applause.

"Even Jackie?" Joel asked, sprinkling hot sauce on his fish.

"Well, she at least fake clapped. She's not so bad. I think that she just needs a friend," she added, sipping sweet tangy lemonade.

"If you say so," he said, recalling the various occasions when they had crossed paths.

Since Mackenzie never had a date, he usually filled in as her escort to any media gala or office party. "Being a shady bitch is not how you make friends. Remember the Christmas gift she bought for you that time she pulled your name from the office pool."

Mackenzie couldn't help but to laugh, remembering the anti-aging creams Jackie had given her along with a card that read: Some things are better left unsaid.

"Yeah, that was petty. Let's not waste our lunch talking about Jackie. What's been happening with you at work these days?"

"Nothing new." He sighed heavily to emphasize how mundane his job felt. Joel Sanders decided the day before graduation that he had no desire to pursue a career in his major, education. He went back to school to earn a degree in interior design. For the past eight years, he made a great living working for a large design firm—which he complained about every chance he got. "Still catering to a bunch of spoiled pill popping white women who change their minds every five seconds."

"I still say that you should start your own firm. You're more than talented enough."

Suddenly, the familiar twinkle returned to his eyes. "So, I just finished decorating this doctor's office in Sandy Springs," he said, ignoring Mackenzie's compliment. "Dr. Andre Lang."

"Here we go again," Mackenzie said, rolling her eyes. "Yeah, you've mentioned him before."

"He is so damn fine. I'm pretty sure that he's in to guys."

"OK, I'll bite. What makes you so sure?" she asked, forgetting that she should never doubt Joel's intuition about these things.

"Trust me, I can tell. He was intentionally making eye contact with me throughout the entire design process."

She chuckled. "So, he's gay just because he was being respectful?"

"I'm serious. Watch what I tell you. I just need a good reason to go back to his office. He's a gynecologist. You know, a doctor just for women."

"You're not fooling anybody. You're trying to get me to volunteer to go get a pap smear or something so that you can come along to harass this man."

"Well, I wouldn't say harass, but could you?" he smiled. "Besides, it wouldn't take too much effort. You know that no one can resist me."

Mackenzie loved him but refused to stroke his inflated ego, even if he were right. Joel was thirty-nine, five-foot-eleven with an athletic body. Dressing well was second nature. Today he wore a maroon power suit, white shirt, and rose-pink tie. A chocolate baby face and a sharp wavy fade highlighted his handsome features. He was all too aware of the magic in his smile that drove both men and woman crazy. He made no attempt to hide his lack of attraction towards the latter.

"I guess," Mackenzie said. "You and your man hunt."

"What can I say?" Joel shrugged unapologetically. "I love 'em. Now what about you? When are you going to get you some? Or at least get out of the house more. Let your hair out of that same ole stale pony tail. 'Cause sometimes I worry about you."

Mackenzie looked up from her lunch. It had been so long since she had seriously thought about being with a man other than Marlon. Joel might as well have been speaking Chinese.

"I'm fine," she said unconvincingly. "I've got my kids and my career to keep me warm."

"Yeah, I know you're fine. I also know that you miss, Marlon. I miss him, too. But don't you get lonely? It's been over three years hasn't it?"

Mackenzie felt that Joel was being insensitive, despite there being some truth to what he said. She often did get lonely, and her body sometimes yearned for the attention of a man.

"I said I'm fine," she said, taking a bite of fish. "Besides, you don't need any competition from me anyway."

Joel chuckled at the thought of him and Mackenzie competing over men. Sensing that the topic was making her uncomfortable, he moved on to a new subject.

"So, you never did tell me about this press conference you're going to."

Mackenzie told him how the Atlanta district attorney had called the press conference to announce the arrest of Thomas Walters in Brazil.

"I know her family is relieved that they may finally get some justice," Joel said. "Rich, white people think that they can get away with anything."

"Well, let's hope that he won't get away with this." Mackenzie glanced at her watch. "Let's watch our time. I don't want to be late."

"OK," Joel said, shoveling down a forkful of macaroni. "I'm going to have to put in extra time on the treadmill tonight, but this cheat meal right here is worth it."

———

Andre entered the examination room to greet a walk-in patient, Cindy Myers.

"Hello, Ms. Myers," he smiled, extending his hand to the young woman casually flipping through a magazine. An oversized tan trench coat swallowed her petite frame. Round, dark sunglasses hid most of her face, and strands of dirty blonde hair tumbled from underneath her khaki plaid fedora. She appeared to be someone who doing her best to be incognito.

"Hi," she replied, ignoring his handshake. She quickly folded the magazine and stuffed it in her purse. Andre noticed that it was one from his office.

"How are you doing to today?" Andre again tried to break the ice.

"Fine."

"Good to know." He got the hint. Her dry demeanor and covert attire conveyed that she wasn't interested in small talk. He would oblige her by getting to the point of her visit. He reviewed her file. "So, you're here to follow-up on a positive home pregnancy test."

"Sure am. And I want to get rid of the thing ASAP."

"You mean have an apportion?"

"Yes. That's what you do here don't you?"

"Yes and no," Andre replied, sitting across from her. "My policy is to only preform apportions in certain situations such as if the life of the mother is in danger, rape or if the fetus is not viable."

"What? Well you should state that on your website, so that you don't waste people's time. The only reason that I'm here is because my usual doctor was booked for the week, and your receptionist said that you could see me quickly."

"My apologies, but I believe that our website clearly states our policy."

"Well I didn't see it," she said as she gathered her things to leave. "Who do I pay for this visit?"

Andre looked at her with sympathy. He had seen women in her situation many times before at his practice in Memphis: A young woman who had gotten pregnant by whatever circumstance and wanted to discreetly erase a mistake. "I'm not going to charge you."

"Thank you."

"You're welcome. Before you leave, Ms. Myers, is there something going on that has you in such a hurry to have an abortion."

"Not that it's any of your business, but I just don't have time for a baby right now," she shrugged. "And since you are unwilling to help me guess I need to find a doctor that will."

"I see," he said. "Look I don't know your situation, but I know that abortion is not an easy choice to make. I can't help you for my own personal reasons, but it is your right." He opened a drawer to get retrieve a brochure for his colleague's practice. Dr. George Mitzner."They may be able to help you here."

"Thank you," she said, wiping away tears from beneath her shades.

He drove past Lang's office one more time. Not too slowly so as not to draw attention. A quarter mile down the road, he parked his car then jogged past the building. A police cruiser slow rolled by. The two officers inside barely noticed him. As far as they were concerned, he belonged in the upscale neighborhood. Despite the hoodie that covered his head. He wanted to check on the progress of his plan. Plans fail without follow up.

Out of the corner of his eye, he saw a young woman exit the building and hurry to her car. She had her head down and looked upset.

He shook his head as she drove passed. *This motherfucker is at it again*, he frowned. Some people just won't learn. Good thing he was a patient teacher. Plans fail without follow up.

The press conference was held in the spacious, glass enclosed rotunda of the Justice Center of Atlanta. Mackenzie walked, in joining a gaggle of eager journalists. She knew most of the people there and some congratulated her on her award. The lobby hummed with crews from all the major television networks, newspapers, and bloggers.

Detective Keith Wilson stood out to her. Over the years, he had become a good friend as well as a reliable source for inside scoops. Mackenzie was attracted to him, though she would never admit it to herself. She brushed off his flirting whenever she worked with him or bumped into him at crime scenes.

As if he felt her eyes on him, Keith glanced over from his conversation with a television reporter. Mackenzie looked away. Too late. Keith excused himself and started towards her. Watching him approach with the confident stride of an African jungle cat, Mackenzie concluded that Keith was especially handsome today. Camera ready. She often mused that if he ever gave up law enforcement, he could easily make a career on the pages of fashion magazines.

Keith was a tall man with milk chocolate skin. His head was shaved nearly bald. A crisp goatee surrounded his full kissable lips, and he had the longest sexiest eyelashes that Mackenzie had ever seen on a man. Always smartly dressed, he wore a tailored charcoal grey suit over a white shirt, and black tie. He body filled out his blazer for anyone to tell that he was well acquainted with the gym.

"The lovely, Mrs. Hill," he said, long eyeing Mackenzie.

Keith thought that Mackenzie was one of the most beautiful women that he knew. Inside and out. She wore her hair pulled back in a ponytail most times that he saw her, but its simplicity only seemed to enhance her features. She wore minimal makeup that showcased her smooth honey-brown skin that begged to be caressed, and her delicate lips invited him to kiss them. Her deep brown eyes were his favorites. "Congrats on your award last night. I don't think that anyone deserved it more. That exposé that you did on how bureaucratic neglect in the state foster care system disproportionately affects African American children was inspiring. I know that it opened a lot of people's eyes to what's really going on."

"Thank you, Keith." She looked at him curiously. "Were you at the ceremony last night?"

"No, I'm sorry," he said. "I wanted to come. I have a couple of other friends in the media who were also honored, but unfortunately the dead bodies never stop showing up."

"Always on duty I see."

"Hey, I've got to be." He grinned. "The bills never stop showing up either."

Mackenzie nodded in agreement. "Amen to that. No breaks." She chuckled. "Keith its good seeing you again but I need to find myself a good place to sit before it gets too out of control in here. You know what sharks us media folk can be, so I'll talk to you later."

She started to walk away. Keith called her back.

"What's up?" she asked.

"Listen, Mackenzie," he said. "If you have any free time coming up let's go out for a drink or maybe even dinner."

Mackenzie was speechless. She realized that Keith was attracted to her, but she never imagined that he would try to take it beyond harmless flirting.

"I...I don't know about all of that Keith," she said, stumbling over her words. She tried to think of a legitimate excuse to decline. There was none.

"Come on, Mackenzie," he coolly pleaded. "It will be just a harmless little dinner between two friends to celebrate your achievement. Nothing more."

He was right, Mackenzie thought. Her conversation that she had with Joel at lunch was fresh in her head. There was no harm in having dinner with him and letting her hair down for a change. Literally. She might even have a good time. "You have my cell. Call me later this week."

"Will do," he said. He tried to hide his excitement, although he was sure he wasn't doing a very good job of it. Mackenzie turned to leave. Keith watched her shapely frame and thought it was hard for him to believe that she was the mother of three.

"What a woman," he whispered.

Mackenzie walked away. She couldn't believe that she had agreed to go out with Keith. He had billed it as a harmless dinner, but the implications meant much more to her. Hell, she still wore her wedding ring. *I shouldn't go through with it.* If he called, it would be best to just brush him off with an excuse about work or the kids. She glanced back. *Poor Keith.* He had seemed so excited and he always bent over backwards to help her out with her investigations. She wouldn't do that to him. It was only an outing between two friends. No different than having dinner with Joel. *Right?*

She looked over at the eager group of journalists. She watched Keith talking to the DA as they approached the podium to proceed with the conference. *A date with Keith Wilson*, she pondered, heading to her seat. *What have I gotten myself into?*

CHAPTER 3

"Good evening, Mrs. Russell." Andre waved to his next door neighbor while checking his mailbox.

"Hey, young man." she waved back. She was loading her car with meals she delivered five nights a week to shut-in seniors—a remarkable task for a woman seventy-seven-year-old woman.

"Do you need any help?" He walked over to her, knowing that she would refuse as usual.

"No, thank you, Doctor. There's still a little life in this old body, you know," she replied, flashing a smile full of dentures.

"Yes, ma'am." Andre smiled. "Have a good evening. "

She halted. "What are you doing for dinner tonight, young man?"

"I hadn't really thought about it. Dinner is usually what looks best on Uber Eats."

She shook her head like a concerned grandmother, disapproving of her grandson's poor eating habits. "I want you to take this." She gave him a plastic container from her cart. "And I won't take no for an answer. There's more than enough. I always make extra."

"Thank you, Mrs. Russell. Smells delicious."

"Wait until you've tasted it," she said, bragging. "Make sure you stop by and see me soon. I miss your company."

"Will do."

Mrs. Russell turned to resume her task.

As soon as Andre entered his house his one-year-old chocolate Cocker Spaniel ambushed him, wagging her nub of a tail and jumping up on his legs. He loved her animated greeting each time he returned to his minimally furnished, low-lit house.

"Hey, Lilly," he cooed, rubbing her belly. "Hey, baby," She followed him to the French doors where he let her out to his small, fenced-in backyard.

While Andre stood in the doorway watching Lilly sniff around before settling on the perfect spot to do her business, his thoughts faded to his first day as a practicing physician in over three years.

All things considered, the day had gone well. He saw several patients, a usual mix of pap smears, UT infections, and women in varying stages of pregnancy. The odd exception was the stealthy young woman that had come in for an abortion. At his practice in Memphis, he would have performed the procedure with barely an afterthought. Today, he simply explained his policy of only performing abortions in extreme cases and referred the mystery patient to a college.

His office manager, Paula, had impressed him by implementing ways to help the business side of his practice run efficiently, down to the last color-coded detail. Paula's professionalism had even convinced him to go with her suggestion of hiring her cousin, Byron, to clean the office at night. Andre had his apprehensions since hiring the relative of an employee had not gone well in the past. Work ethic aside, he did find her to be somewhat strange. Over pious. Not that piety was a bad thing, just that Paula Easton conveyed hers with a touch of fire and brimstone zeal. He was perplexed that as devout as she came across she would want to work where the manifestations of sin could be clearly seen each day.

The house phone rang. He answered the anonymous call, expecting that it was probably just a telemarketer. Instead of an annoying sales person's voice an eerie computerized one spoke.

"You-made-a-mistake…You-made-a-mistake" the voice said, sounding out each word in robotic monotones, quickly followed by the dial tone.

Andre stared at the receiver as if he could see the words floating from it for him to decipher. *Mistake? What was that all about?*

Lilly ambushed him from behind carrying her food bowl in her mouth, demanding to be feed.

"Hey, girl. You hungry?" He laughed, dismissing the bizarre call as a wrong number. "Let's go see what Mrs. Russell gave us to eat."

––––––––

Thanks to the relentless traffic on the highway, Mackenzie didn't arrive to Nate's house until a little before 6 p.m. She saw his dirty Tahoe in the driveway parked next to his wife's minivan.

The house was well lit on the inside. Mackenzie could see through the bay windows that the twins were in the family room playing video games with their cousins, eight-year-old Nathan Jr., and seven-year-old Jarvis. Nate lay stretched out on the couch on his iPad. His five-year-old daughter, Ayana, drew in a sketchpad on the coffee table. Traci sat Indian-styled on the carpet with her nose in a book. Mackenzie didn't see Beverly, but from the smell, she was in the kitchen whipping up a culinary masterpiece that she had seen on the Food Channel.

Mackenzie had to ring the doorbell twice before Beverly answered with the usual judgmental expression on her chubby face. Beverly was a stay at home mom who was completely submersed in domestic bliss. Like Mackenzie's mother, she disapproved of the amount of time and energy Mackenzie devoted to her career. She was always trying to fix Mackenzie up with the 'perfect' guy she knew from church.

"Hey, Bev, Mackenzie smiled. "How's it going?"

"Antwan's teacher said that he got a fight with another boy over a game or something. So, you need to talk to him."

"A fight?" Mackenzie said, surprised to hear that one of her boys was fighting. "I will to talk to him. Thanks Bev."

"Don't mention it. That's what family is for." Beverly said. "Kids don't raise themselves, you know."

Mackenzie ignored Beverly's attempt to remind her that she was a neglectful, career driven, mother. "What's on the menu. Smells good in here."

"Roasted rosemary chicken, garlic mashed potatoes, and asparagus. We'll have a nice family dinner about five minutes."

She joined the rest of the family lounging in the family room. She flopped down on on Nate's lap.

"Whatcha' doin', big bro?" she said, teasing him like she did when they were kids.

Nate was two years older than Mackenzie and a male, six-foot version of her. They had the same nice features and honey-brown skin. Growing up, Nate was always bigger than most kids in his class so naturally he levitated towards sports. Football in particular. After high school he attended the University of Georgia on an athletic scholarship. He was dubbed the next Herschel Walker by numerous NFL scouts, until a car accident during his junior year shattered his kneecap along with his promising football career.

Crushed, Nate refocused on finishing his degree in mathematics. After college, he taught high school math, settling for coaching the school's football team. Despite that setback, Mackenzie knew Nate had no regrets. He loved working with kids and would probably still be teaching today if the burgeoning needs of his own family had not required him to return to school for his MBA. He presently ran a successful CPA firm.

"Get off of me." Nate laughed, pretending that Mackenzie was too heavy for him.

Mackenzie pulled up his grey UGA T-shirt to poke at his belly.

"Looks like you could use a treadmill for Christmas." She teased him.

"Never mind that," he said, pulling down his shirt and patting his stomach. "This comes from my wife's good cooking."

Mackenzie looked down at her pigtailed niece, Ayana, who was giggling at the childlike exchange between her father and aunt.

"Ain't your daddy fat?" she asked her, kneeling to Ayana's level for a kiss. Ayana giggled and nodded in agreement.

"Beverly," Nate yelled, laughing. "They're ganging up on me in here."

"Leave my baby alone," Beverly shouted back.

If anyone else in the room noticed that Mackenzie was there they made no indication. The boys lay on their stomachs transfixed by their video game. Traci, highlighter in hand, was equally transfixed by her biology book. When Mackenzie spoke to her she answered with a barely audible "Hey, mom" and a wave, never once looking up.

Mackenzie sometimes worried about her daughter. She was born the first-year Mackenzie and Marlon were married. Marlon was an only child, so he had hoped to have a big family. Because of complications during Traci's birth, the doctor told them that Mackenzie would possibly not be able to carry another child to term. Despite that disappointing prognosis, the twins arrived eight years later.

This is what troubled Mackenzie. Traci was stuck in the middle. She was too old to relate to the young kids in the family, and mature for her age, too young to really relate to the adults. Mackenzie encouraged Traci to get out more with kids her own age but outside of the occasional outing or two, Traci chose to stick mostly to herself and her books.

Mackenzie made her way over to the boys. She cleared her throat to get their attention. Rashad, Nate Jr., and Jarvis glanced away from the TV just long enough to manage a quick hello. Antwan did his best not to make eye contact with his mother. Mackenzie knelt down beside him.

"Excuse me, sir. Are you Mr. Floyd Mayweather Jr.?" she whispered, trying to make him laugh. Mackenzie didn't believe in making her children feel any guiltier about their actions than needed.

Antwan turned to her with his best puppy dog-face face. "I didn't start it, mommy," he said, pouting.

"We'll talk about it later, boo," she said with a hug and a kiss to his forehead.

Beverly peeked into the room and announced that dinner was ready. Mackenzie took Antwan by the hand. "Come on, Auntie Beverly made you some of those mash potatoes that you love so much."

After enjoying the lasagna Mrs. Russell had given him, Andre stretched out on the couch. Lilly slept on the floor next to him. The TV was tuned to the evening news. Everything was the same. African-American activist protested police brutality, people suffered from natural disasters, school shootings were the norm, and terrorism threatened the world.

Strangely, the dismal state of the world reminded him of Rene. She was a champion of the underdog, giving her all to stand up for others. When she invited him to volunteer for charity work or attend protest events, he was always too busy or too uninterested to go. He exhaled a deep sigh of regret then instructed his virtual assistant to turn off the TV and turn on Maxwell.

Before long he dosed off, dreaming of Rene and Zhuri. The recurring dream started off with him, his wife, and daughter surrounded by family enjoying a festive Thanksgiving dinner. Andre started to moan, tossing and turning as the pleasant dream progressed into a ghastly nightmare.

Rene and Zhuri suddenly vanished from the dinner table. He started a frantic search for them, charging through doors that led nowhere, running down hallways that never ended. The nightmare ended the same each time—he found them in his bed, naked and butchered. After he broke down to his knees, they would sit up screaming: *"You let us down. You let us down,"* before bursting into flames.

This time there was a change to the nightmare's ending. Rene and Zhuri kept repeating, *You made a mistake. You made a mistake,* echoing the weird computerized voice from the phone call he had received earlier.

"Rene," Andre yelled, jolting straight up, sweating and gasping for air.

Shaken, he went to the bathroom to splash cold water on his face. He looked at himself in the mirror. His eyes were bloodshot and his usually vibrant, light-brown skin was clammy. He noticed Lilly's reflection in the mirror as she sat in the doorway. She had her head to the floor looking up at him with big brown eyes that seemed full of sympathy.

He turned to her. "What am I going to do, Lilly?" Ears perked, Lilly sat up barking as if to say, *How in the hell should I know?* Andre chuckled. "Come on, girl. Let's go for a walk. We both could use some fresh air."

CHAPTER 4

By midweek, Mackenzie had doors literary shut in her face, transfers to voicemail, and given the general run around while attempting to get an exclusive interview with Thomas Walters. She was over it, especially since she had started the week off with a sunny outlook. She was looking forward to Keith's phone call and the promise of a night out. Luckily, he called her on Thursday evening as she was watching the twins and Nate's boys at football practice.

"Guess who beautiful," he said in his smooth baritone.

"I'm sorry. Who is this?" She teased him.

"The new man in your life."

"Is that right? Well, I'm sorry, sir. You'll have to be more specific than that. There are several new men competing for my attention." She couldn't help but to laugh at that exaggeration. "What's going on Keith? How are you?"

"I'm pretty good. You?"

"I'm OK. A little frustrated with work, though."

Tell me about it. "Well let me help you out with that a little. I'm calling to make good on my offer. I know that it is short notice, but Jill Scott is at the Fox Theater on Saturday. And that new restaurant, Prism, over in West Midtown is very nice. They have great live bands, too."

"Oh really? Are you inviting me, Mr. Wilson? I love Jill Scott."

"Only if you are accepting, Mrs. Hill." He smiled.

"Maybe. But how do I know you that you're not going to run out on me to chase down a killer?"

He laughed. "No police work. I promise. So, are you in? I'd love to show you a good time, Mackenzie."

"I'd like that too, Keith." She finally admitted to him and herself.

Keith was momentarily taken aback. "Great. Concert's at seven on Saturday night. Is that good for you?"

"Sounds good."

"Cool. I'll text you tomorrow to finalize everything."

"OK."

"Bye, beautiful."

Mackenzie immediately texted Joel. In predictable Joel style, he invited her over for a drink to celebrate the end of her 'extended dry spell.' She told him that there was nothing to celebrate. The only thing she would be doing with Keith was enjoying Jill Scott's performance and hopefully have fun and good conversation over dinner. But that she'd come over to his place later for a glass of wine anyway.

Joel lived alone in a gentrified area of Atlanta known as Grant Park. He had transformed a rundown 1940's two-bedroom craftsman into a three-bedroom dream home.

She didn't bother knocking before using her spare key to his house. Joel was in his den stretched out on his sofa wearing only flannel sleep pants. He was watching *"Game of Thrones"*, eating crab dip on club crackers, and washing it down with red wine. An explosion boomed on the TV and he shouted: "Damn, that bitch Cersei is crazy!"

Mackenzie moved his feet to make room for herself on the sofa. "Hey, boo. I'll take this," she said, seizing his glass.

"I literally just poured that." Joel protested mildly, then went to retrieve another glass from the small bar he had setup. "So, tell me about this man who has got you all giddy."

"His name is Keith Wilson. He's a sex crime detective with the APD. You've seen him before."

"I have?" He resettled next to her and poured himself a replacement glass of wine.

"Yeah. I've pointed him out to you a couple of times whenever he was on TV."

"Ok. Yeah, I think remember him. Tall, brown skin dude. He's very attractive."

"Ain't he though?" Mackenzie gushed like a schoolgirl. "And that body." She lay back on the sofa and flung her legs across Joel's lap.

"Look at you," he smiled, taking sip of wine, happy to see his friend more upbeat than usual. "So where is he taking you?"

"To see Jill Scott at the Fox theater on Saturday. He also said something about dinner at this place called Prism in West Midtown. Ever hear of it?"

"Yeah. I haven't been there yet, but I know someone from the design firm who decorated it. I heard it's nice. Very cosmo. Expensive too. Mr. Wilson must really be trying to get some, huh?"

Mackenzie rolled her eyes. "I'm not ready for all that Joel."

"Um. I think that ole thirsty miss kitty cat is the one that's going to make that decision," he laughed, clawing at her crotch.

She hit him with a pillow. Sometimes Joel could be so crass. "Pass me that damn crab dip."

As hard as she tried, by Friday Mackenzie was full of so much nervous anticipation that she was unable to concentrate on work. She had a legitimate excuse since this would be the first time she had gone out on a date with a man, other than Marlon, in over eighteen years. Giving up on getting any work done, she opted to take the rest of the afternoon off to do a little pre-date shopping. Mackenzie decided to bring Traci along and use the time to tell her about Keith.

Mackenzie parked behind the queue of empty buses outside of Excelsior Preparatory School. The bell had just rung, so a few students were making their way through the doors. She was just about to send Traci a text when she saw her strolling hand-in-hand with a tall boy wearing a blue and white basketball uniform. He gave Traci a peck on the lips before darting back into the school. Mackenzie was shocked. Her little bookworm was growing up and obviously had some parts of her that life Mackenzie knew nothing about.

She blew the horn. Traci came up to the car window with a *Please-don't-tell-me-you-saw-what-I-think-you-saw* look on her face.

"Hey, mom. What are you doing here?" she asked.

"I took off early today," Mackenzie replied, giving no indication that she saw anything out of the ordinary. "I thought you might want to go to the mall."

After a 20-minute run, Mackenzie sank into her spa tub. Lavender scented bath oil filled the room and pampered her body. The twins were at Nate's for the weekend. Traci was at her high school's basketball game. *A basketball game*, Mackenzie chuckled. Traci had never showed any interest in sports in the past. Mackenzie pictured her on the bleachers cheering on the young man she had spotted her with.

It seemed like only yesterday that Mackenzie and Marlon had brought Traci home from the hospital. Now she was nearly sixteen and had a *secret* boyfriend. Yesterday, while shopping, Mackenzie told her about Keith and the hang-ups that she was having about dating again. Traci said that she was glad that Mackenzie was finally doing something other than working or worrying about her and her brothers.

With the usual maturity beyond her years, she had reminded Mackenzie that her dad would want her to move on with her life. She had even helped Mackenzie pick out a chic khaki green jumpsuit, perfect for an evening with Keith.

Mackenzie was glad that her daughter had reacted in a positive way, but she was disappointed when Traci didn't share anything about her mystery boy. Mackenzie wanted to ask her about him but held back figuring that Traci had her reasons for secrecy. Mackenzie trusted her daughter. She knew Traci would open up when she felt that the time was right. She was confident that whatever Traci was doing, she was being smart.

Mackenzie set the tub's massage jets for thirty minutes. Keith called earlier to say that he'd be over around 6:00, giving her a couple of hours to unwind before she needed be ready. She closed her eyes and sank deeper into the water. Something told her that tonight was definitely going to be interesting.

CHAPTER 5

He sat across from the trendy hookah bar watching her loud drunken laughter with her friends. They were snapping group selfies before saying their goodnights. *She looked younger than twenty-five,* he thought. A pretty girl with blonde hair, big tits, and nothing much on her mind other than partying and shoes. Which was why she had an abortion— too busy to think of anyone other than herself, much less a child. She probably didn't even give her boyfriend a say so in the matter. Selfish bitch. They were all alike.

He had spent most of week shadowing her, waiting for the perfect time to make his move. He needed to use her to reiterate a point to one, Dr. Andre Lang, a man who did not learn lessons well. Seeing her approach, he ducked out of view. He knew that she was headed for her little green Mini Cooper parked on a dark residential street away from prying eyes. Waiting until she had passed, he got out to follow her, making sure to close his car door quietly.

Her expensive high-heels clip-clopped, as she reached her car, keys in hand. She heard him approach. On instinct, she pointed a stun gun on her keychain at him.

"Stay back. I'm not afraid to use this," she shouted, hoping that someone heard her.

"Hey. Don't shoot. I'm harmless," he said, smiling and holding his hands up. "I'm lost and I was hoping you could help me out. I'm looking for this club called WAR around here. It's supposed to be *the* spot on Saturday nights. Have you ever heard of it?"

"Ye…yes, I have," she stuttered between shallow breaths, continuing to hold her stun gun at arm's length. Her trembling hands easily betrayed her brave front.

He smiled. "Good. Could you show me how to get there? I promise I'm not a psycho. I just moved here from Richmond, Virginia a month ago and I'm still having trouble keeping up. Atlanta is so big."

"Oh, really? Richmond?" she said. She warmed to his boyish smile. Suddenly, he didn't seem so threatening. *He's actually kind of cute,* she thought, lowering her weapon. "I'm from Richmond, too."

He leered directly into her eyes. "I know," he stated darkly, sending a shiver down her spine.

Realizing that letting her guard down was a fatal mistake, she tried to react. Her effort was in vain. With a force that would have put down a man twice her size, he caught her with a hook to the chin. She stumbled back against her car—instantly knocked unconscious. He quickly scanned the area to see if there were any witnesses. Satisfied that there were none he used her keys to unlock her car door, callously shoved her limp body into the backseat, then jumped behind the steering wheel.

Yeah, Dr. Andre-fucking-Lang needs a history lesson, he sneered, leaving in her car. The lesson that Lang had forgotten in Memphis, he would make sure that it was impossible for him to forget again.

––––––––––

"So, what do you think?" Keith asked Mackenzie while they were seated in the vestibule of Prism waiting on the hostess to show them to their table.

Mackenzie surveyed the crowded restaurant. It occupied a restored 19th century warehouse and was decorated with vibrant colors and chic decor. A massive glass, backlit bar monopolized half the room. Festive patrons were seated at tables that bathed them in a sexy glow. Music flowed from a stage in the rear, featuring a live neo-soul band jamming in front of morphing video projections on the walls. A crystal chandelier sparkled from the center of the ceiling crowning it all.

The atmosphere was electric. Urban. Prism was energized with upwardly mobile couples like Mackenzie and Keith, who had just come from seeing Jill Scott's awesome performance.

"I think it's fabulous," Mackenzie replied, grooving to the music. "Very cosmo."

Before Keith could respond the hostess, a young lady with long auburn dreadlocks, appeared just as the band announced that they would be taking a thirty-minute break. With a bubbly smile, she introduced herself as Niki and asked them to follow her. Granting Keith's request for something out of the way, she seated them at one of the tables near the back of the restaurant. .

"You two make a cute couple," Niki commented, offering them menus.

Keith winked at Mackenzie. "Don't we?"

"We're just friends," Mackenzie politely corrected her.

Niki apologized for her assumption, then offered them drinks on the house. The restaurant's signature rum *Pink Pussy Passion* was her suggestion. Mackenzie gladly accepted. Not one for fruity drinks, Keith just wanted Tequila on the rocks.

"Gotcha," Niki said. "Be right back."

They both thanked her.

Mackenzie further took in the restaurant's ambiance and décor. She caught a glimpse of their reflection in one of the beveled mirrors lining the exposed brick walls. Keith was as handsome as ever, dapper as always in a black Dashiki with detailed bronze embroidery. Mackenzie had her shoulder length hair styled in soft curls. Gold hoop earrings framed her face. The khaki green jumpsuit that Traci had help picked out hugged her shapely figure, spruced up by a pair of python Louboutin pumps.

Niki's right, Mackenzie thought. *They did make a nice couple.*

Niki dropped off their drinks.

"So, are you enjoying my company so far?" Keith asked.

Mackenzie reached for her drink. He noticed that her wedding ring was missing. It had been present since she stuck a recorder in his face two years ago, inquiring about a homicide case. *Interesting,* he thought. Keith understood that she would never be completely over husband's death, but the absence of her ring suggested that she was at least ready to try moving forward with someone else.

Mackenzie took a sip of her drink. "So far, so good," she said. "I have to admit. I was kind of nervous about this evening. It's been a long time since I've been out with a man like this. I honestly didn't know how I was going to act. Silly right?"

"Not at all."

"I'm really enjoying myself tonight. Thanks for inviting me, Keith."

Keith leaned forward, gazing into her eyes. "My pleasure, gorgeous. Thanks for coming," he said, rubbing the back of her hand.

Reflexively, Mackenzie pulled her hand away, knocking over her drink. Embarrassed, she grabbed a napkin to wipe it up. Keith reached for his napkin to help. The waiter also helped and offered to replace Mackenzie's drink. She accepted and ordered an ahi tuna. Keith ordered the grilled salmon entree.

As soon as the waiter was out of earshot Keith said, "I apologize if I made you uncomfortable."

"No, you didn't do anything wrong, Keith. It's just that I…" Mackenzie froze in awkward silence to find the words to reassure him.

Keith stepped into rescue her. "It's OK, Mackenzie. You don't need to say anything else. I understand. Now tell me some more about those kids of yours. Rashad, Antwan, and Traci, right?"

"Yes. Six-year-old twin boys, and a fifteen-going on thirty-year old daughter. They're the center of my world," she said. "But let's talk about you. I feel like the conversation has been dominated by my dull life all night."

"You know that I don't mind," he smiled. "But, as far as my life goes, I think that you probably already know all there is to tell. I'll be forty in May. I grew up in Troy, AL, the middle child of three boys. I went to Tuskegee for undergrad and Florida State for grad school and earned a master's degree in criminology. I've been with the APD for about fifteen years. That's about it. Ole boring me. Never married. No kids. Just the job." Keith paused, then added. "But, I'm hoping to change all of that soon."

"I didn't know you—" Mackenzie started, then she got sidetracked. She could have sworn that she saw Joel. "—had a master's degree," she finished, continuing to survey the area where she thought she spotted Joel. She was right. It was Joel. He was sitting four or five tables up toward the front of the restaurant with some guy. He seemed to be trying to hide his face behind a menu while spying on Mackenzie and Keith. Realizing that he was busted, Joel waved to her, an embarrassed grin on his face.

Keith noticed that she was distracted. "Who's caught your eye?" He turned to see his competition.

"Nobody really. I just spotted a friend," Mackenzie replied, pointing in Joel's direction.

Joel mistook her gesture to mean *come on over*. He did of course, leaving his date to guess what was going on.

"Small world," Mackenzie said, giving him a knowing look.

"Yeah it is," he said, leaning over to hug her. "I forgot to mention that I had planned on coming here tonight, too." He pointed at his temple. "They say the mind is the first to go."

"The mind, huh?" Mackenzie squinted at his transparent lie. She looked over at Keith. "Keith this is my best friend, Joel."

"Nice to meet you," they both said, shaking hands.

"Love your Dashiki, Keith," Joel said. "Very stylish."

"Thanks, man."

"So, are you two kids having a good time?" Joel asked. "I heard that the concert was phenomenal."

"It really was. Jill really shut it down tonight," Keith replied.

"I'm pissed that I missed her. My date and I were trying to get tickets, but they were sold out." Skipping further small talk, Joel went straight to the point of his snooping. "So, Keith, what do you guys plan on doing after you leave here?"

Mackenzie cut in. "Uh, Joel, shouldn't you be getting back to your date?"

"Hey, I have an idea. You and your lady friend should join us." Keith offered, ever the gentleman. "Where is she sitting?" He looked around expecting to see some lovely woman sitting alone waiting for Joel's return.

Joel looked at Mackenzie, his eyes asking her what he should do. Mackenzie only gave him a 'you got yourself in this mess' shrug. On cue, Joel's date appeared at their table introducing himself as, Todd. He excused himself, and asked Joel if he wanted him to go ahead and order their food.

Keith's eyebrows furrowed. He looked at Mackenzie for answers.

"Um. You know what, Keith," Joel said. "Thanks for the offer, man, but Mackenzie's right. We don't want to impose. You guys have a good night. Call me later, Z." Joel told Keith it was nice meeting him and shuffled Todd back to their table.

The entire exchange was a straight out of some clichéd sitcom: "*Joel and Mackenzie.*"

"OK…That was strange," Keith said.

"That's just Joel. Strange sometimes. But he is my closest and dearest friend. You'd like him a lot if you knew him."

Mackenzie could tell that Keith wasn't satisfied with her explanation. He continued watching Joel scurry away with his date. Joel must have told Todd some fabricated excuse of why they had to leave, because they left a few seconds later. Keith's look of disgust told Mackenzie that he had it figured out and he did not approve.

"So, your friend's a faggot, huh?" he asked with disdain rolling off his tongue.

"Excuse me?" Mackenzie frowned. "Keith, please do not use that kind of language to describe my friend. Yes, he is gay, but that doesn't mean that you get to insult him."

Keith sensed that he had struck the wrong nerve with Mackenzie. He hastily tried to recover. "I apologize, Mackenzie. It's just that in my line of work whenever I come across those kinds of people they are usually promiscuous perverts. Even child molesters. Since I joined the sex crimes unit, I can't begin to describe all the sick things I've seen those people involved in. Or worse, how many times I've had to bust a monster that has raped an innocent little boy. You're a journalist. I know you've seen the same types of things. You can't tell me you leave Joel alone with your twins. Plus, I don't think that someone like him would be a good influence on them."

Mackenzie glared at Keith, fuming as she heard the words coming from his mouth, not believing that he was the one saying them. Although, she had defended Joel's sexuality many times during their friendship, this time she didn't know what to say. The sincere, sensitive gentleman who had so gallantly charmed her all evening had vanished. In his place sat a bigoted man that she never would have given the time of day had she known that he harbored those kinds of feelings.

Never one to create a scene she calmly collected her thoughts before she spoke.

"Yes, Detective. As a journalist in this city, I have seen firsthand the horrible things done to children by sexual predators. But you cannot lump gay men into the same category as pedophiles. And certainly not Joel. Yes, I leave him alone with my boys. He's bathed them, changed their diapers, kept them on weekends. He is their godfather. They love him and I trust him with their lives." Mackenzie angrily added, "And for the record, my husband felt the same way."

Keith's rebuttal was halted first by the waiter returning with Mackenzie 's new drink, then by his chiming cell phone. He wanted to ignore it so that he could get back to redeeming himself with Mackenzie, but it emitted several beeps that obviously meant urgency.

"I'm sorry, Mackenzie. I have to take this call."

Mackenzie heard him scold the caller about disturbing him the one night he had asked not to be bothered. When Keith's angry whispering abruptly ceased, and he paid attention to Parnell's every word, Mackenzie knew that the call was warranted. Somewhere in Atlanta a poor soul had lost their life. Violently. Keith concluded the conversation by assuring Parnell that he would be there ASAP. "Mackenzie, I apologize," he said. "I know that I promised no police work, but something has come up." He waved their waiter down to inform him that they needed to leave.

"It's alright, Keith," Mackenzie replied, standing. "I think the night was over anyway."

———————

The activity at the center of Piedmont Park was what Keith had seen too many times. Blue lights flashed, several squad cars served as a barrier to the crime scene, partitioned off with yellow police tape. Frustrated and cursing himself as he walked through the park, Keith glanced back at Mackenzie sitting in his car, sitting haphazardly on the lawn.

Driving over from Prism, he had offered her his most sincere apology for insulting her friend. She accepted it without any fanfare, but he could tell that she was upset. Probably more from disappointment than anything else. The evening had been going so well. He could tell that Mackenzie was beginning to let her guard down. Genuinely enjoying his company until he ruined everything by being an asshole. Now walking alone on the damp grass toward yet another homicide scene, he hoped that he hadn't blown his chances with her.

Keith had to push through the crowd, which included a mixture of news reporters or residents of the park's affluent neighborhood demanding answers. Uniformed police officers tried to keep everyone at bay.

At the heart of the commotion he saw his partner's lanky frame in jeans and a grey Morgan State University sweatshirt. He was talking with the medical examiner as they stood over the body of a nude, white female laying face up in the grass. A forensic photographer was busy documenting the scene.

"Mr. African GQ himself," Parnell said, seeing Keith approach.

"One night. I asked to be left alone for one little night, Parnell," Keith said, flinging his hands skyward. He acknowledged the medical examiner and photographer with a nod.

"Sorry man. I wanted to handle this myself, but this shit right here is your territory." Parnell maneuvered a flood light over the victim.

Sex crimes were Keith's specialty, and this victim had definitely been sexually assaulted. To what extent he didn't know. Keith crouched down to get a better view of the body; flung on the lawn like a discarded rag doll. She was in her mid-twenties, shoulder length blonde hair, and a petite build. There was a large bruise on the left side of her face. Red ligature marks seared into her wrist and ankles indicated that she had been tied down. What stood out the most were the brutal lacerations seeping a small amount of blood from her stomach. "The killer definitely wanted her dead," Keith said to no one in particular.

Keith stood as his years of training and experience kicked in. He turned to the medical examiner, a short balding man, who was scribbling notes on a small pad.

"Any idea how she died?" Keith asked him.

"Well, I wouldn't want to speculate on a cause of death without an autopsy. However, I'm fairly certain that she was dead before she was sliced open like that." He pointed at her gashes with his pen.

Keith turned his attention back to Parnell. "Who found her?"

"Someone called 911 a couple of hours ago. Claimed she stumbled over the body while walking her dog. No name. Prepaid phone," Parnell stated.

"Any chance we've got an ID already?"

"Not yet, boss. We took prints. I've already got someone from missing person looking for a possible match."

"Good." Keith refocused on the victim. He shook his head at the familiarity of it all. DEATH. This word had permeated his life for so long that sometimes death seemed to be all that life was about. At times, Keith had to remind himself that life had much more to offer. One day soon he planned on finding out just what. "Parnell, I've got a feeling that this shit right here is going to get a lot worse before this is all over."

"Keith." He heard someone call.

Keith turned to see Mackenzie trying to cross the police tape but was being held back by an officer.

"I see why you didn't want to be bothered. Damn, she's fine." Parnell pointed out. "My bad, dog."

"Shut up, man." Keith said, starting toward Mackenzie.

"What's happening, Keith?" she asked him.

He led her toward his car, explaining that a body had been found in the park.

"I'm going to be here all night, so I'll have an officer take you home if you don't mind?" he asked with regret in his voice.

"No, thank you," she said. "I'll manage. I assumed that something major was going on, so I already requested an Uber." As if hearing its cue, a grey Toyota Camry approached, stopping when Mackenzie waved it down. "Well, here's my ride. Goodnight, Keith." She turned to leave. He reached out to stop her.

"Mackenzie, again I'm sorry about—"

Mackenzie held up her hand. "No need to apologize again, Keith. Really. I do think that you were wrong, but I'm not going to hold a grudge against you. I just hope you get better educated about the LGBT community."

Keith held out his hand. "Still friends?"

"Still friends," she said, giving him a firm handshake. "Goodnight, Keith."

He opened her car door. "Goodnight, Mackenzie."

"Oh, and I expect an exclusive on this story, right?" she said, stepping into the back seat.

"You've got it."

She waved at Keith before the car sped off. He rejoined the homicide scene, regretting that he had to exchange her company for a dead body in the middle of Piedmont Park. The smart, funny, sophisticated, and beautiful, Mackenzie Hill. She was type of woman he could see himself settling down with. The type of woman he had hoped would be his reason for leaving all this death behind.

CHAPTER 6

"Traci, you're going to miss your bus!" Mackenzie shouted to her daughter. Traci had been locked in the bathroom longer than usual.

"I'll be out in a minute, mom," Traci called back.

She wiped away tears, trying to keep her voice from quivering. She sat on the edge of the tub, wondering what in the world she was going to do next. It was three weeks since she had first made love to Antonio. Three weeks since that morning when they had carelessly not used a condom. They had decided that it was best to use them from that day on. Staring at the results of a home pregnancy test that she had purchased to confirm why her period was late, it was clear that their efforts had come too late.

PREGNANT. The word resounded loudly in her head. She was now a statistic. One those girls who had to drop out of school eventually ending up on welfare. An appearance *Maury Povich* would soon follow.

"Traci," her mother called again. "What are you doing? You know you've got school."

"I'm coming."

Going to school was the last thing she wanted to do. She preferred to stay locked in the bathroom forever with her shame. She texted Antonio him that she needed to talk to him ASAP, then threw the pregnancy test in her book bag. She double-checked to make sure that she did not miss any incriminating evidence before leaving the bathroom.

Her mother was waiting at the bottom of the staircase. The twins were standing next to her, bundled up in matching black pea coats. Traci self-consciously descended the stairs convinced that all eyes were on her and that everyone knew her secret.

"Are you feeling OK?" Mackenzie noticed Traci's slightly bloodshot eyes.

Traci looked at her mother. She wanted to fall into her arms and confess everything: Antonio, skipping school, having unprotected sex, the pregnancy test. Her mother would know what to do.

"Yeah. Just cramps," she lied instead.

"Are you sure?" She checked Traci's forehead with the back of her hand for fever. "I've got some Midol if you need it."

"I'm OK, mom," she said, going around Mackenzie. "I'm going to miss my bus if I don't hurry." Traci practically ignored the twins on her way out front the door. She walked down the driveway, pulling the hood of her coat over her head to make herself as inconspicuous as possible.

"Traci." She heard her mother call from the opened garage door, ushering the twins into the backseat of the car. Traci turned to face her.

"You know that you can come to me about anything."

Her mother's words carried an omniscient meaning.

"I know, mom," Traci replied, continuing her path, fighting back tears. *I know.*

"I've got to get back to work, but for the last time it was not your fault," Mackenzie said to Joel, slightly annoyed.

Since that comical night at Prism, Joel felt compelled to apologize to her every other conversation. Mackenzie tried to brush the whole thing off by saying that she and Keith just didn't click. Joel still insisted on believing that he was the reason. He was not actually at fault, but Mackenzie didn't have the heart to tell him all that had really happened.

"That's what you keep saying, but I just feel so bad. I saw how in to him you were before I had to sashay my black ass over to your table. And that look on his face when Todd came over. Lord knows what he said after we left. And I know you would have jumped to my defense."

"Joel," Mackenzie said sternly, switching the phone from one ear to the other as she pulled a file from her briefcase. "The only thing that happened when you left was, Keith got an urgent phone call and we had to leave. Amiably. No hard feelings. No mention of you. I've told you this several times and I know that you've seen those news reports about that girl who was found murdered in Piedmont Park. So please stop. You're feeling guilty for nothing. Not to mention getting on my nerves."

Joel persisted. "Yeah. Yeah. I know what you've told me. And how could I possibly miss the story about that girl?" he said.

Everyone in Atlanta knew about Dana Bradford's rape and murder. She was a twenty-five-year-old professional that had met her end and the crime had the wealthy Piedmont Hills community up in arms, demanding the immediate arrest of whoever committed the atrocity in their neighborhood. "And I'm not stupid, Z. You and Keith went out almost two weeks ago. If you and him are so amiable, how come you haven't mentioned speaking to him since?" Joel paused. "Hold on a second. I have to take this call."

The line went silent. Mackenzie thought about what to tell Joel when he came back to the phone. The truth was she did speak to, Keith. Mackenzie knew his true reason for calling was to gauge her attitude toward him after their date, but he said that he was just calling to give her an off-the-record exclusive about the homicide as he had promised.

Her friends, family, and co-workers had described her as a selfless, hard working girl without an enemy in the world. It was speculated that Dana's murderer was a sexual predator who followed her from the hookah lounge, then raped and strangled her to death in the park. A terrible scenario in itself, but apparently there had been much more premeditation to the crime than the police were willing to release.

The autopsy report showed that Dana had been sexually assaulted, however she did not die of an impulsive strangulation. The medical examiner inferred from a nasty bruise on her face, ligature marks on her wrist and ankles that someone had first knocked her unconscious to subdue her. She was then taken to a different location where she was raped while her extremities were tied. After which, she was deprived of air using a plastic bag. As if this were not enough, Keith had saved the most gruesome detail of Dana's demise for last. The killer or killers performed a ritualistically horrific act on her: They slashed open her abdomen and ripped out her uterus.

Keith's graphic account of what may have happened almost brought Mackenzie to tears. Dana Bradford died alone. She died in an ungodly manner straight out of a horror movie. Her remains dumped in Piedmont Park like a sack of garbage. Mackenzie pictured Dana stretched out on a bed, begging for her life. She understood why the police wanted to withhold this information from the public. They did not know if they had a serial killer on their hands and they certainly did not want to inspire any copycats.

Joel had to call Mackenzie's name twice before she realized that he was back on the line.

"I'm here," she said, shaking Dana from her thoughts.

"Sorry for the hold and for bringing up the whole Keith thing," he said. "I don't mean to keep beating a dead horse. It's just that I want so badly for you to be happy. It kills me to think that I may have come between you and a potential relationship."

"I appreciate that, boo. Really, I do. But you didn't come between anything. Keith and I had one insignificant date that just didn't go anywhere. Besides, Keith ain't the only fish in the sea, you know."

"Yeah, but you're getting too old to be fishing. "Pretty soon no one is gonna go after your dried up old bait."

"Ha, ha very funny."

"Just joking," he chuckled. "You know that you're a timeless beauty. I've got to go. There's a client on hold right now ready to complain, so I'll talk to you later."

Joel hung up, leaving Mackenzie to attempt to concentrate on her work. Useless because she was too preoccupied with the same thought she had before Joel's phone call: Traci. Mackenzie had seen her daughter deal with cramps enough times to know that cramps were not the sole reason for her grim mood this morning. Mackenzie speculated that Traci might be having a problem with her boyfriend. Maybe it was something more. She decided to confront Traci, tell her that she knew her secret, and hope that Traci wouldn't shut her out. They always had such a close relationship and Mackenzie didn't see why it should not continue to be that way.

"Knock, Knock." Mackenzie looked up to see her editor, Mr. Montgomery, poking his gunmetal hair through her office door.

Even this early in the day, he had the top button of his striped oxford shirt undone, the knot of his blue tie slacked several inches from his collar, and his sleeves rolled up to his elbows. Robert Montgomery had the unmistakable appearance of a self-made man who worked every bit as hard as he did thirty years ago, when he had founded the Atlanta Star. Thanks to his direction it one of the largest black-owned daily newspapers in the country.

"Come on in," Mackenzie said. She eased her laptop close, embarrassed that she had not typed a single word in about thirty minutes.

"Hard at work on that next award I see." Montgomery smiled.

"I'm trying my best."

"That's the spirit," he said, sitting down. "Listen. I want to do another angle on the Walter's story. Tell me what you think."

"OK."

"Let's do a story profiling the DA, prosecuting the case, the presiding judge, and the Walters' lead defense attorney. It would be a split page kind of deal with a shot of both counselors on either side of the judge. We'll call it: 'Dueling Counselors' or a 'Tale of two Lawyers' or something. I'm not good with headlines. Anyway, what do you think, Mackenzie?"

"Good idea, chief. Then after that maybe we can use the same format for a profile story on both families involved, the victim's, and the accused."

"Exactly," he said, springing to his feet. "I know that it's short notice, but why don't you get to work on this angle immediately for Sunday's paper. Come to think of it, you're going to need help on this one, so I want you to work with Jackie."

"Great. I'll get right on it," Mackenzie said through the phoniest smile that she could muster.

He left her office, and she thought, *work with Jackie, huh?* Mackenzie cringed recalling the few times she had worked with Jackie had been like pulling teeth. They had co-authored superb pieces in the past, but Mackenzie felt that they could have accomplished more if Jackie didn't constantly treat her as a rival. Mackenzie grabbed a pen and pad and headed for Jackie's office. She greeted several co-workers with a smile or hello along the way.

Jackie's door was closed as usual, but Mackenzie could still make out her distorted figure through the frosted glass door. She was sitting motionless at her desk. Mackenzie gave the door two short knocks. No answer. After another knock, Mackenzie heard Jackie's raspy voice tell her to come in. She opened the door expecting Jackie's usual caustic greeting, but instead she found Jackie slowly massaging her temples. It was obvious that Jackie had been crying.

"How can I help you, Mackenzie?" she asked not making eye contact.

Jackie the ice queen crying? Surely the world was coming to an end with a bombardment of fire and brimstone.

"Um, Montgomery asked me to run this idea for a story by you. He suggested that we work on it together."

Jackie wiped her eyes and cleared her sniffles with a tissue. "OK. Have a seat. What is the idea?" she asked unusually civil.

Mackenzie sat. "It's about the Walter's trial—but you know what, Jackie? I can just come back later if it's a bad time."

"No. I'm fine. Allergies."

"OK, because if I can help or even if you just need to talk to someone about something, I'm here for you."

Jackie rolled her eyes. "Talk?" she hissed back to her lovable self. "Don't give me any of your magnanimous BS, Mackenzie. You don't like me. I don't like you. But we have a job to do. So, let's just do it as quickly as possible so we can get out of each other's face. Now, what is the story idea?"

Mackenzie shook her head. She was used to Jackie's bad attitude, but this time there was something more. Pain.

"That's not true," Mackenzie said, making sure her voice was not patronizing. "Not at all. I don't have any ill feelings toward you, Jackie. And I'm not on some Oprah, sanctimonious kick either. You just seemed upset. I—"

Jackie cut her off with a dismissive wave.

"Ok. Tell you what. The next time I'm feeling like throwing myself into rush hour traffic, I'll make sure to remember that you're a goddamn therapist on the side." Jackie snapped. "Now, I'll ask you again, Mrs. Hill. What were you saying about a story idea?"

Mackenzie did not persist. She would simply do her job as Jackie had insisted. What was she thinking anyway? Tears or not, this was still Jacqueline Smalls that she was dealing with: World Class Bitch.

———————

Joel whipped into Lenox Square Mall's parking lot driving much faster than he should. He didn't care. Traci said that she had taken the train there and that she was waiting for him in the food court. After hearing how upset she sounded, he didn't want to keep her waiting long. She had called while he was on the phone with Mackenzie crying about something that she needed his help with. Something that she could not go to her mother about. Growing up in Philadelphia with two sisters, he instantly recognized that as code for drama.

Joel beat an old lady in a Cadillac out of a parking spot, ignoring her shouting and horn honking as he rushed toward the food court entrance. Traci was sitting in the front far off from the noisy lunchtime crowd. She was looking just as dejected as she had sounded over the phone. She saw him approach and quickly stood to embrace him. In his arms, she was his little goddaughter again. Sobbing, innocent and helpless with a boo-boo that only Uncle Joel could kiss to make better.

"Shhhh," he squeezed her tight. He sat down with her and pulled several napkins out of a dispenser to wipe her eyes. "What's this all about?"

"I'm pregnant, Uncle Joel," she blurted out.

Joel lingered on her declaration for a moment, sorry that his first inclination had been correct. This was drama. He hugged her again.

"OK," he said. "Why do you think that you are?"

Traci lifted her book bag from the floor and sat it on the table. She unzipped it.

"My period was late, so I used one of these this morning," she replied, sliding it closer to Joel. He peeped inside and saw an opened home pregnancy test sitting on the top of Traci's books. He smiled a little inside. The situation might not be so bleak after all.

"Traci, those things aren't always accurate. Just ask your moth—"

Traci stopped him before the word *mother* could hit the back of his teeth.

"No. Please, Uncle Joel. I can't go to my mom with this. Not yet."

Joel tried to reason with her. "But Traci, you shouldn't keep something like this from your mom. I think it's best that we tell her now. Mackenzie is a lot more understanding than you may think."

"That's not what I'm worried about," Traci said. "I just don't want to bother her. At least until I know for sure. I know that she's had it kind of hard since my dad died. She's just started trying to move on and I know she needs me to help her out. Not cause more problems."

With sympathy, Joel looked into his goddaughter's bloodshot eyes. Everything that she was feeling became clear to him. Traci was only about twelve when her father died, but she sometimes took on adult responsibilities. Joel could recall when he would stop in to check on them only to find Mackenzie in her dark bedroom, balled up under the covers.

On days when Mackenzie could barely will herself out of bed, Traci insisted on helping Mackenzie's family make sure that the house was cleaned and that the twins never missed a diaper changing, or meal. Traci became her mother's helper as well as her protector. Joel understood why Traci was reluctant to go to her mother. To Traci a teen pregnancy meant that she was now a burden.

Joel decided to do it Traci's way for the moment.

"OK, Traci, first things first," he sighed, taking charge. "We need to find out if you're really pregnant." Traci nodded in agreement. "Secondly, what about the father? Who is he?"

Traci told him that the young man in question was Antonio Osborne, a basketball star at her school. They had known each other since elementary school, and that she had been secretly dating him for about eight months.

"We're in love," she said.

In love, he scoffed, remembering a basketball player he thought he loved when they were in high school. Joel thought the feelings were mutual, but the only thing Joel was to him was a secret little experiment. *Those damn basketball players will get you every time.*

"OK, have you told him, yet?"

"No. I was going to this morning, but I got scared. I skipped school and came here instead. I didn't know what to do, Uncle Joel, so I just walked around until I called you."

"I'm glad you did," he said with a consoling smile. "So, I guess we better see about getting you to a doctor." *Doctor.* Joel snapped his fingers remembering the very handsome client that he had a few weeks back. He pulled out his phone to find the number for Dr. Andre Lang.

"Who're you calling?" Traci asked.

"Someone who might can help. You know your mother is going to kill me when she finds out about this," he warned Traci as the phone rang. "Dead."

CHAPTER 7

"There's your baby girl," Andre said, pointing at the ultrasound image materializing on the screen. He ran the Fetal Doppler along his patient's swollen stomach. "There's her tiny little heart beating, and she's got all her fingers and toes. Mrs. Lopez you've got yourself a healthy little princess. We should meet her in about three months, or so."

"Three more months, huh? *¡Dios mío!*" My God. The chubby, Puerto Rican woman sighed. "Isn't there something we can do to speed up the progress?"

Andre smiled. "Nope. 'fraid not. I thought you'd be used to this by now. This is your third child, right?"

"Don't remind me, doctor," she said, adjusting her clothes. "Nine months of total discomfort with each one. I tell you, someone should invent a pill to keep you numb the whole time."

"You don't mean that," he replied, making indications on her chart. "The little discomfort that you endure only makes you more appreciative of the little angels you've given birth too."

Mrs. Lopez squinted at him as though he were crazy. The knowing look of a mother with two young boys. "Angels?" She laughed. "You and your wife must not have any kids, Dr. Lang."

"No, no children," he said aloof from having his daughter stolen. "No wife for that matter either."

Mrs. Lopez's expression changed to disbelief as she looked at her doctor. He was an exceptionally good-looking man. Kind of skinny for her taste, but the bulges underneath his shirt promised a nice chest.

"You're not married, doctor? I can't believe some lucky girl hasn't snatched you up. Wait. Are you gay?"

Andre laughed at her bluntness. "No, Mrs. Lopez. I'm not gay."

"Because if you are, I have a cousin that I can fix you up with," she said, showing Andre a picture from her cell phone. "He's cute, right?"

Andre glanced at her phone. "Yes, but, no thank you, Mrs. Lopez." He turned and paged his PA, Ciara. "Ciara, can you come finish up with Mrs. Lopez for me, please."

Ciara appeared. He handed her the chart then turned his attention back to his patient. "I want to see you back here next month, until then keep eating right and taking your prenatal vitamins."

"Yes, doctor and don't forget about my cousin if you change your mind." Mrs. Lopez said with an impish grin.

"Goodbye, Mrs. Lopez," he said, leaving the examination room.

Andre chuckled to himself as he walked toward the front of the office. He was used to people playing matchmaker once they found out he was alone. Usually it was a sister or girlfriend they wanted to hook him up with, never a gay cousin.

He stopped at Paula's desk to make sure that Mrs. Lopez was his last patient before heading out to lunch. Paula was standing in the waiting area with her back to him having a heated discussion with a tall man. Noticing Andre patiently waiting for them to conclude their argument, the man indicated Andre's presence to Paula with a nod in Andre's direction.

Paula jerked around. "Oh. Excuse me, Dr. Lang," she said.

"That's OK, Paula. I was checking to make sure you didn't have anyone scheduled before I took off for lunch."

"No, sir. Mrs. Lopez was the last. Your next appointment is at 1:30." She gestured towards her guest. "Dr. Lang, this is my fiancé, Christian Terry."

"Oh. Your fiancé?" Andre was surprised to hear that Paula even dated, much less had a fiancé. "Nice to meet you, Christian."

"Call me Chris. Nice meeting you too, doc. Nice set up you got here," he noted wildly shaking Andre's hand. "I've heard a lot about you. Thanks for treating my Paula here so good."

Andre considered the narrow-faced young man with sweaty palms and wide, crooked smile, standing next to tiny Paula. As always, Paula was the picture of piety in an ultraconservative gray ankle length skirt that swallowed her and a pink blouse buttoned all the way up her neck. She never wore anything remotely considered revealing, kept her brown hair in a tight bun, and not a hint of makeup ever graced her pale face. She was a sharp contrast to her husband to be. Tall and lean, dressed in a black leather jacket and ripped jeans, Christian Terry had the appearance of a man whose visits to church were few and far between. They certainly seemed to make an odd couple. The secular gigolo verses the devout church mouse.

"I should be the one thanking you," Andre replied, discreetly wiping his damp hand on his pant leg. "Paula's a God send around here."

Chris pulled Paula close to him. "That's my girl." He grinned.

Ciara emerged from the examination room followed by Mrs. Lopez, who waved goodbye as she left.

Andre checked his watch. "Well, I've got to get something to eat guys. Real nice meeting you, Chris." Andre took steps toward the door but was stopped by Ciara calling for him to wait.

"We have something for you, doctor. Don't leave yet."

She hurried to the back. Andre looked to Paula for some clue as to what was going on. She only gave him a coy shrug that suggested that she knew more than she was willing to tell. After a moment, Ciara retuned carrying a small vanilla frosted cake with a red number forty shaped candle on top.

With no joy, Andre remembered that it was October 12th, his birthday. Since he fought hard to suppress feelings like his life had ended the day he lost his family, Andre's birthday was one of usually happy occasions that he cared not to remember.

Paula started off a cheery round of *Happy Birthday*.

In a flash, Andre was back in Memphis celebrating his surprise thirty-seventh birthday party, Rene had thrown for him. The last celebration they ever had together.

He could see Zhuri's smiling face holding an elaborate chocolate frosted cake, yelling, "Surprise daddy," when he walked through the door. He could hear the festive singing and cheers from friends. Most of all, he could feel the enduring love that he had for his wife and daughter burning every bit as bright it did three years ago today.

When they finished singing Ciara sat the cake down in front of Andre.

"Happy Birthday, Doctor Lang," Ciara smiled, pulling him back to the present.

"Thanks, Ciara. Thanks, Paula," Andre said after he blew out the candle. "I really appreciate you guys going through all this trouble for me. I've been so busy that I forgot today was my birthday."

"No trouble at all," Paula said. "I noticed that it was your fortieth birthday while I was filing some paperwork for you. I thought we had to do something to celebrate."

The phone rang. Ciara volunteered to answer it since she said she had to get plates and utensils for the cake anyway.

"So, you're the big 4-0 today." Chris grinned. "How do you and your wife plan on celebrating, Doc."

"No wife," Andre said for the second time that day.

"You're kiddin' me. A good lookin', successful guy like you?"

Paula shot Chris a look that he either did not see or just ignored.

"No. Not kidding."

"Oh, well. Maybe one day," Chris said. "So, did you make a wish?"

Andre half-smiled. "No, not this time."

"Too bad," Chris said. "I know that doctors make all kinds of money, but there must be *something* that you want." He winked at Andre. "Maybe the perfect lady."

Andre unintentionally made eye contact with Chris. He saw a coldness that made him uncomfortable. Thankfully, Ciara came back in the room with flatware. She informed Paula that she had left the information on the caller who needed an appointment for tomorrow on Paula's desk. A Mr. Joel Sanders.

Joel Sanders? Andre pondered the familiar name, trying to place it with a face. He remembered, just as Paula was handing him a large piece of cake. Joel was the hilarious, interior designer that worked for, Southern Elegance. *Why would Joel need the services of a gynecologist?* Andre wondered, shoveling a piece of cake into his mouth out of politeness to Ciara and Paula.

"Thanks again guys. Thanks very much."

———

"Thanks, Bev. See you tomorrow." Mackenzie beeped and waved at her sister-in-law.

She backed out of the driveway, braking once to make sure that the twins were securely buckled up in the back seat before heading home. Mackenzie was anxious to see Traci. On the way over to pick up the twins from Beverly, Mackenzie had heard a disturbing voicemail from Traci's homeroom teacher, Ms. Harris. She had called to check up on Traci since she had missed a couple of days from school.

When Mackenzie texted Traci to find out where she was, Traci responded that she had just gotten home from her after school science club meeting. *Unbelievable.* That was not like Traci. It was definitely time to have a serious talk with her. Mackenzie didn't need any more evidence to know that there was something going on with her daughter much more serious than menstrual cramps.

As soon as Mackenzie opened the door the twins plowed past her to the refrigerator, grabbed a snack, and raced to the family room. Mackenzie followed her nose to the pleasant smell coming from the kitchen. Traci was standing over the stove nursing a simmering pot, looking considerably more upbeat than she had been this morning.

"Smells good, Sweet T," Mackenzie said, peering over Traci's shoulder. "Whatcha' got going there?"

"Hey, mom," she replied, smiling. "Just some baked chicken, yellow rice, and vegetables. I thought I'd cook us dinner tonight." Traci cut opened a package of frozen broccoli, then dumped its contents into the steamer. "How was your day?"

Mackenzie caught herself. She was about to tell Traci that she had seen better work days. The last-minute assignment that Mr. Montgomery had given her wasn't the problem, it was the dealing with Jackie's bad attitude that had added unnecessary tension to her day. But, Mackenzie couldn't concern herself with that now. She wasn't raising Jackie.

"Fine. The usual," she said dryly. "What about you? Are you feeling any better?"

Traci downplayed her mother's concern with a nonchalant chuckle. "I'm fine, mom. I told you that it was just cramps."

"Are you sure that was all it was?" she asked, giving Traci another chance to come clean. "You seemed really down this morning."

"Everything is cool, mom. Really."

Mackenzie looked at her daughter pretending as if everything were peachy. She treated her concern as a simple case of motherly overreactions. Mackenzie could feel herself getting vexed mixed with a heavy dose of disappointment. She had heard stories from friends about their unruly teenagers and had always felt blessed that Traci did not behave that way. Maybe the credit belonged to the values that she and Marlon had instilled in her early on. Maybe Mackenzie had just been taking Traci's *good girl* demeanor for granted. Either way, this was a moment that Mackenzie was not prepared for. Her baby girl was lying to her.

"I know that you have been skipping school, Traci. Your teacher called," Mackenzie said.

Traci continued to focus on dinner, avoiding eye contact with her mother.

Mackenzie interrupted her as she started to speak. "Before you say anything let me say this. I don't know all the details, but I can pretty much guess that what's going on has something to do with that boy that I saw you kiss that day I picked you up from school. Now I want the truth. What's been going on, Traci?"

Traci started crying. Disturbed by the sight, Mackenzie couldn't help but tear up, also. She embraced her. "What's wrong, Traci? You can tell me."

"I'm pregnant," she whispered.

Mackenzie couldn't say a word. Traci's unbelievable declaration sent her mind reeling. She made her way over to the breakfast nook. Traci followed, taking a seat across from her.

"Tell me everything, Traci," she finally said as an ache creeped in the back of her head.

She listened intently as Traci recounted all the events of the last few weeks. Her relationship with Antonio. Skipping school. Forged doctor's excuses passed off to teachers. Unprotected sex. The positive pregnancy test. Her frantic plea to Joel for help. Joel setting up a doctor's appointment for her. Every detail. All of it unreal, none of it what she had come to expect from Traci.

Mackenzie struggled to suppress an urge to yell and do all the things she vowed to never do as a parent. Instead she only let out a long hard breath.

"Traci, can you go up to your room for a while? I really need a moment to process all of this."

Traci sat still, staring at her mother as if trying to read her mind. "Are you mad at me mom?" She sobbed.

"Mad? No, I'm not mad, baby." She wiped the tears from Traci's eyes with her thumb. "I would be lying if I said that I wasn't disappointed. But no matter what I will always be here for you. In the meantime, please just go to your room. I'll be up to talk to you soon."

Traci left to do as her mother had asked.

Mackenzie sat drumming her fingers on the table, wondering: Where she had gone wrong? What she could have done to prevent this? She figured that her first action would be to call Joel to get the information about the doctor's office and go from there. She called him well aware that he had played a willing part in Traci's deception. She knew that Traci had probably forced Joel's hand by playing on his soft spot for her. And while now was not the time to go off on him, Joel was still going to get an earful. Mackenzie had to take her frustrations out on somebody.

CHAPTER 8

Keith walked through the district attorney's office, greeting people he cared not to know with half-smiles. He had been summoned by ADA James Connors about the Thomas Walters case. From Connors' agitated voice over the phone there was some bad news. Keith had come to expect nothing less.

Keith hard knocked on Connors door.

"Come in," ADA Conners said.

As soon as he entered the tight matchbook office the smell of musty underarms and drug store cologne slapped in the face him.

"What's going on?" Keith asked.

ADA Connors looked up from shuffling through a filing cabinet. The sloppy mountain of a man's clothes had obviously been fished from a dirty clothes hamper. There was no mistaking where the musty smell came from.

"Detective Wilson," he said. "We're going to need to find more evidence on the Walters case before trial."

Keith shook his head. "What else do you need to get a conviction? We've have witness testimony that Walters was the last person to be seen with her and DNA evidence. This should be a slam dunk case."

"The judge threw out the DNA. Seems the chain of custody was compromised."

Keith glared at Connors. "How the hell was there any kind of break in the chain of custody? I logged it in myself."

Connors shrugged like it wasn't his problem. "Hey that's what the defense argued and the judge ruled in their favor. You want to take it up with the judge? Be my guess."

Keith stormed out of the office, slamming the door behind him. *I'm so sick of this shit.*

The day after finding out that Traci may be pregnant, Mackenzie sat with her in the North Atlanta office of Doctor Andre Lang, observing her surroundings in silence. A serious looking receptionist sat behind a counter multitasking. There were three other women of various ethnicities in the waiting area. All three were noticeably pregnant. One was with a young man who was probably her husband. They were laughing, joking, and flipping through baby magazines. A cute, young couple. They reminded Mackenzie of her and Marlon when they were bright-eyed, newlyweds expecting Traci, vowing to afford their children every opportunity. A teen pregnancy was never part of their plan.

Mackenzie looked at Traci. Her expression was just as down as Mackenzie would expect. She was fifteen and about to find out if she was about to become a mother. Not to mention if she had contracted any STDs. Mackenzie tried not to think about that. She had spoken with Antonio's parents to let them know what was happening and to drill them about their son's past sexual habits. God forbid he had given Traci anything.

Mr. and Mrs. Osborne did not seem exactly shocked that their sixteen-year-old athlete son was sexually active, but did express concerns that he was being reckless by not using condoms. They promised to have a talk with Antonio and offered to support Traci in any way that they could.

After about ten minutes of waiting a curvy young woman, wearing her hair in tight coils, came into the waiting area. She called Traci's name. Mackenzie stood with Traci, holding her hand to reminded her that she would always have her back. The young woman introduced herself as Ciara, Dr. Lang's physician's assistant. She escorted them to an examination room. Ciara had Traci sit on the table and she skimmed over the clipboard that she was carrying. Mackenzie sat on a stool next to her.

"I see that you are here for a pregnancy test and an STD workup," Ciara said.

Traci looked to her mother for confirmation. Mackenzie nodded.

"Yes," Traci whispered.

"OK. How many days have you been late?"

"About three or four," Traci replied.

Ciara made indications on her chart. She sensed how nervous Traci was. "OK. Four days does not necessarily mean that you're pregnant."

"I took a home pregnancy test. It was positive," Traci said, staring at the floor.

"Well, that doesn't necessarily mean that you're pregnant either," Ciara said. "But, we well find out for sure." Ciara again referenced her chart. "So, have you ever had any STDs or been tested for HIV in the past six months?" Traci shook her head. "OK. Well, now I'm going to take your vitals and draw some blood, then the doctor will be in shortly."

"OK."

Ciara took Traci's vitals, then drew three vials of blood from her left arm. She placed a small bandage over the puncture when she was done.

"That wasn't so bad was it?"

"No." Traci tried to smile.

"Cheer up. I'm sure that everything will work itself out," Ciara said, giving them both a reassuring smile as she left. "Dr. Lang will be in a moment."

Mackenzie got up and sat next to Traci. She placed her arm around her shoulder. "Ciara is right, you know. Everything will be fine. No matter what I'm here for you."

After a brief wait Mackenzie heard a preppy male voice in the hall talking with Ciara. She assumed that it was Dr. Lang coming in to examine Traci. When the muffled conversation ceased, the doctor walked in.

Even though Mackenzie's mind and heart were completely focused on Traci, it would have been hard for her not to notice that Dr. Lang was a handsome man. He was about 6"1' with a nice, athletic physic and radiate light brown complexion. He wore his hair faded and his sculpted face framed with a low neat stubble . A black, cashmere V-neck sweater over black gingham shirt, purple tie and grey slacks complimented his good looks. Mackenzie could see why Joel was so taken by him. Dr. Lang had an inviting air about him.

"Miss Traci Hill. Mrs. Hill," Dr. Lang greeted them with a movie star, white smile. He extended his hand first to Traci, then to Mackenzie. "Hello, I'm Dr. Lang."

Mackenzie noticed that both his gentle handshake and his liquid brown eyes lingered with her a few seconds longer than necessary. She didn't mind at all.

"Hello," they both replied.

"I thought Joel Sanders was bringing Traci in today," he said.

"That's a long story." Mackenzie sighed.

Dr. Lang smiled knowingly. "How is ole Joel? I was looking forward to seeing him."

Mackenzie rolled her eyes, still somewhat irritated with Joel for his part in Traci's dishonesty. "He's fine. Same ole, Joel."

"Yeah, I can imagine," he chuckled, shaking his head. "Joel did a fantastic job, but I had a time with him when he decorated my office. He's a real character. Tell him I said hello the next time you speak to him."

Mackenzie acknowledged his request with a humorless grin.

Dr. Lang again referenced the file. "OK. Now back to the reason for your visit today. Ciara did most of the work, but I just need to go over a few things with you." Dr. Lang proceeded to ask Traci a battery of questions, some of which Mackenzie had to answer.

Traci asked him when the test results would be in.

"I'll definitely know the results of your pregnancy test tomorrow afternoon. As far as you STD workup goes, Traci, it can come back tomorrow also if the lab doesn't have to retest a positive result. If that happens it can take up to two weeks." He noticed Traci shrink in defeat. "Honestly, Traci, I have a feeling that everything will come back normal." Dr. Lang turned to Mackenzie. "Tell you what Mrs. Hill if you leave a contact number upfront with my office manager, I'll call you personally with the good news."

"Thank you," Mackenzie said.

"No problem at all. I know how nerve-racking these things can be," he said, patting Traci's shoulder. "It was very nice meeting you both, and I'll be in touch with you tomorrow. Have a good day ladies."

Mackenzie's drive home was quiet, partly because the twins were still at Nate's. It was a school night, but she had allowed them to stay over a little longer so that they could play video games with their cousins. The other reason was because Traci had barely uttered a word since they had left Dr. Lang's office. She only slumped against the car door, staring out of the window as if she could see her future passing her by, ignoring Mackenzie's attempts at cheering her up.

Arriving at the house, Mackenzie was surprised to see a boy wearing a blue Excelsior Preparatory School lettermen's jacket sitting on her stoop. If Mackenzie didn't instantly recognize him, the look on Traci's face would have said it all. He was an infamous young man —a significant contributor to her headaches. Traci jumped out of the car to confront Antonio faster than Mackenzie could put it into park.

She demanded to know what had possessed him to show up at her house. Antonio's sincere reason was that he was worried about Traci since she had not come to school for the past two days. He also said that his parents were pissed at him about what was happening, so he was afraid to go home.

Mackenzie got out of the car, watching their exchange. God forbid that Traci was pregnant, but their offspring would be a beautiful child. Antonio, dark brown with bedroom eyes and chiseled features. He was just as handsome as Traci was pretty. Mackenzie cleared her throat to get their attention.

"So, you are Mr. Antonio Osborne," Mackenzie stated without the slightest hint of a smile.

"Yes, ma'am," he replied, offering his hand. She overlooked it. She was in no mood for pleasantries.

"Get in the car, young man. I'm taking you home. We've got some serious talking to do with your parents."

CHAPTER 9

Andre reviewed the results of Traci Hill's pregnancy test and STD workup. He was pleased that everything came back negative. Traci was such a sweet young lady. She reminded him of his daughter. STDs aside, Andre hated to think of the complications a pregnancy would have brought into her life. Traci could have chosen to keep her baby, sacrificing much of her youth and freedom. She could have given the child up for adoption and probably to regret for the rest of her life. Opting to have an abortion would have surely heavily burdened her young psyche.

He looked up the information to call Traci's mother as he had promised. Andre reflected on meeting her yesterday. In hindsight, he realized that he had been staring at her a little too hard. It was unprofessional behavior even if Mrs. Hill didn't seem to notice or care.

Andre was surprised that Mackenzie had invoked that kind of reaction from him. He had kept that part of himself under lock and key since Rene's death. At the urging of his family and therapist, Andre had tried relationships with a couple of other women. They all failed. He wasn't ready. The pain was still there, the memories too strong. Outside of the rare casual hookup, he chose to remain alone not willing to pull another woman into his emotional void.

He dialed Mackenzie's number. She picked up on the first ring.

"This is Mackenzie Hill," she answered.

"Hello, Mrs. Hill, this is An—Dr. Lang. How are you today?" He could practically hear her heart stop.

"Hello, Dr. Lang. I'm good. Been better," she said with nervous anticipation.

"I can imagine," he sympathized. "Well you could put your mind at ease," he told her without preamble. "Traci is not pregnant. No STDs. She's completely fine."

"Thank God." she exhaled. "Why did the home pregnancy test show positive? I thought that those tests were fail proof."

"Well, I wouldn't exactly call them fail proof. It might have been an expired test. Also, Traci might have actually been pregnant when she took the test, but for whatever reason the embryo doesn't attach to the uterine wall. It's pretty common and nothing to worry about. Either way, she is definitely not pregnant."

"Thank you doctor for getting back to us with the results so quickly."

Andre was happy to be the one to deliver to the good news.

"Not a problem. Like I said, I know how troublesome this situation can be. Of course, Traci should do a follow up STD checkup in about six months just as a precautionary measure, but she should be fine," Andre paused. "Mrs. Hill, I don't mean to pry, but may I ask you a question?"

"Of course."

"Have you and your husband spoken with Traci about the importance of safe sex. Better yet, abstaining all together. She's a terrific girl. I'd hate to see her get caught up in a preventable situation. I've seen it happen too many times."

"Well, I'm raising her alone," Mackenzie replied. "My husband passed away. But you're right. I'm a journalist and I've done enough stories on how teen pregnancy and STD's are running rampant in the in the black community to know what you mean. I spoke to my daughter about it. Apparently not as in-depth as I should have, though. Traci has always been so mature for her age that I guess I took for granted that she would know better."

"I'm sorry, Mrs. Hill. I didn't mean to offend you or imply that you were negligent in your parental duties."

"No offense taken, doctor," Mackenzie said. "Do you have children?"

Andre hesitated. "My only child passed away when she was about Traci's age," he said aloud for the first time in a long time. For some reason, he felt at ease talking to Mackenzie about it. A kindred spirit of sorts.

"I'm sorry to hear that." She recognized the sorrow in his voice and regretted that she had asked him the question.

"Yeah, it's hard to deal with sometimes. But hey, that's what my expensive therapist is for. As a matter of fact, I'm pretty sure that I'm responsible for her getting that new Jaguar," he joked, trying to lighten the mood. Andre knew how easily he could turn the tone of any conversation into depressing when his daughter or wife were mentioned.

Mackenzie was not amused. She wanted to ask him how he is wife were coping with the unimaginable loss of a child, but she refrained. She was nothing if not tactful.

"Give me that number," she chuckled following his lead. "I could use a couple of couch sessions myself."

Andre laughed. "Hey, whenever you're ready. She gives me discounts for referrals."

"There you go."

"But hey, Mrs. Hill I'm going to let you get back to work. Call me if you have any more questions, and please make sure that you do that six-month follow-up."

"Definitely. Thank you, Dr. Lang."

"You're welcome. Goodbye."

———————

Mackenzie hung up the phone, slumped back in her chair, relieved that Traci had dodged a bullet. One of the two six-hundred-pound gorillas had been lifted off her back. Now she had to figure out how to handle the other. Specifically, what she was going to do about Traci's relationship with Antonio. There was no way she could knowingly allow her teenaged daughter to continue in a sexual relationship.

Last night when Mackenzie and Antonio's parents had briefly discussed the possibility that Traci might be pregnant, Antonio adamantly professed his love for her. He vowed that he would be there to support Traci and his child. He planned on marrying her. Mackenzie and the Osbornes had almost snapped. They let him know how ridiculous he sounded. What did a sixteen-year-old kid know about love and marriage? And how would he possibly provide for a wife and child?

His simple fanciful solution was that Traci and the baby would move into his parents' house until he graduated high school. There was no doubt that he would be drafted straight into the NBA just like Kobe.

Just like Kobe, Mackenzie rolled her eyes. She didn't have the energy to debunk Antonio's foolproof plan. Besides, there was really no point in discussing the issue until they knew conclusive results.

Thank God the results were negative, Mackenzie exhaled, calling Traci's cell phone.

"Mom," Traci replied. She went right to the point. "What did he say?"

"You're not pregnant." Mackenzie was glad to report that. "You don't have any STDs either."

Traci was relieved. "I'm sorry for putting you through this, mom."

"You don't have to be sorry, Sweet T, that's what I'm here for. I'm just sorry that you felt that you couldn't come to me first. This isn't over Traci. Not at all. We still have a lot more to discuss when I get home. Your brothers are going to spend the weekend with Nate and Beverly, so we will have the house to ourselves."

"I won't be there when you get home, mom. Remember? I promise to babysit Anya for aunt Beverly," Traci replied, reminding Mackenzie that her sister-in-law had recently enrolled in real-estate school. Mackenzie had applauded Beverly's effort to add something more to the monotony of pot roast and PTA meetings in her life. "I plan on taking Anya to the movies, so Aunt Beverly is going to pick me up from the house and drop us off at the theater in Camp Creek. She said she gets out of class at seven, so I should be home around eight. OK?"

"Do you plan on meeting anyone else there, Traci?" Mackenzie pressed her, suspicious that Antonio was the part of Traci's plan that she had conveniently left out.

"No, mom."

"Do you promise?"

"Yes, mom. He has a game in Macon tonight anyway."

Mackenzie begrudgingly relented since Traci had already promised Beverly. "OK, but as soon as you get home we will discuss the consequences of your actions, your relationship with Antonio, your punishment for skipping school, and lying to me. Understand?"

"Yes."

"I love you."

"I love you too, mom."

Mackenzie sighed. Punishing Traci was something she didn't like to do. The last time she could recall was when Traci was seven. Full of scientific curiosity even then, Traci had mixed together household cleaners in a bucket to see what would happen. The first time her experiment failed, and she got off with only a warning. Defiantly, Traci tried again this time producing a nasty gas that left her wheezing, coughing up blood, and ended with a trip to the emergency room. She was punished by confiscating the beloved junior microscope set that Marlon had given her.

Effective punishment for a seven-year-old, but how do you discipline a young teen girl involved in a sexual relationship who had been skipping school, lying, and almost gotten herself pregnant by another teenager with major hoop dreams. This time there was no warning to give, or microscope to take away. And how useful would telling Traci that she could no longer see Antonio be when they attended the same school? Probably shared a lot of the same classes.

Mackenzie glimpsed Marlon's picture on her desk. As much as she missed him as her husband it was times like this that reminded her just how much she needed him as a father to help guide their children. She thought about calling her own parents for advice. She called Joel instead.

Located in the hip East Atlanta village district, Blu Cantina was a quasi-upscale, Mexican tapas restaurant, featuring a rooftop patio. Atlanta's upwardly-mobile singles sought it out in droves for happy hour to network and brag about their latest status symbol purchase. The crowd was just building when Mackenzie arrived to meet Joel. He was late, so she sat alone at the downstairs bar, deep in thought, sipping on a glass of Sangria.

Several guys approached her with corny pickup lines, subtly flashing keys to expensive cars and shiny watches. Mackenzie cordially brushed them off with a polite smile and a show of her wedding ring. One particularly short guy didn't get the hint. Convinced that detailing the dysfunctions of his family life would garner him the sympathy vote, he rambled on about how his wife cheats on him and his kids disrespected him. He pulled out his big guns when he said that he made over $500,000 a year that he was more than willing to lavish on Mackenzie.

Joel came up behind him. Instantly recognizing Mackenzie's distress, he transformed himself from gay best friend to jealous husband, a guise he used to rescue her from love sick men many times before.

"Is this guy bothering you, honey?" Joel asked in his deepest baritone as he stared the man down.

Mackenzie struggled to contain her laughter. "No, sweetheart. He was just leaving." The guy apologized and scurried away. "I'm already mad at you and you have the nerve to be late?" Mackenzie told Joel.

"Sorry, Z. Traffic," Joel said, sitting next to her. He motioned for the bartender and ordered a margarita on the rocks. "So, tell me. Am I going to be a god-grandfather?"

"No. Not right now anyway."

"Whew."

"You can say that again," He took a long swig of the drink that the bartender had set in front of him.

"So, everything is fine?"

Mackenzie sighed. "As far as that's concerned, but I'm a horrible mother."

"Girl, shut up. What are you babbling about?" Joel asked, rattling the ice cubes in his glass. "I need a bigger drink."

"Lush."

He chuckled. "You try staying sober after dealing with her majesty, Mrs. Gloria Bernstein, and her three yapping fur balls for the past five hours."

"Who?"

"Just a client. Nobody important. Why do you think that you are horrible mother?" he asked.

"I failed her, Joel. I knew that Traci had a secret boyfriend, and I said nothing to her about it. What kind of mother lets her teenaged daughter sneak around having sex while, her best friend helps her set up doctor's appointments?" Mackenzie pinched Joel's arm. "Don't think about that I forgot by the way."

"Ouch. I said was sorry." He laughed. "Seriously. I can sympathize with you for about one second, but then I remember that you're a fantastic mother. You know that. It can't be easy raising three kids alone. And I don't see how you could have prevented Traci from doing what she did. She was going to do what want she wanted to do. I mean, how old were you the first time you screwed?"

"Excuse me? I was a virgin until the day I married, Marlon."

Joel nearly spit out his drink. "Lies." He laughed. "Please don't make me name names up in this place. You know that I kept notes of your pre-Marlon exploits, and you were no angel at CAU."

Mackenzie laughed along with him, then her mood quickly snapped back to gloomy.

"I took Traci's maturity for granted, Joel. I did. I should have drilled the virtues of abstinence in her head over and over again. Especially in this day and age. Now what do I do about Antonio?

Follow her around school all day? Take away her phone and computer?"

"Trust me, Z. Traci is scared. She won't be doing the nasty again anytime soon, or at the very least without protection. She's learned her lesson."

"I don't know about that, Joel. You can't un-ring a bell once it's rung."

"Have you spoken to her about it?"

"Not in detail, but I will tonight. Right now, she is babysitting Nate's daughter at the movies. When she gets home, I have the unpleasant task of punishing her, and I don't even know where to begin."

"You can begin by taking a switch to her butt." Joel smiled. "Seriously though, you will figure out what to do."

"Yeah, but I'll hate doing it."

"Every parent does. Wait. I take that back. Every parent except for my mother. I think she enjoyed it. Matter fact, you should give her a call. She gives classes on Tuesdays and Thursdays."

Mackenzie laughed. "Hey, I forgot to tell you that Dr. Lang asked about you. He sends his hello."

Joel's eyes widen. "Really? He is a cool guy, right? And didn't I tell you that he was fine as hell?"

"You did, and you were right. For a second, I thought you were right about him being gay also, but he told me he had a daughter."

He rolled his eyes. "Please you of all people should know that don't mean jack," he said, eyeing a running back built guy that was cruising past with his eyes trained on Joel. Joel nodded at him and the guy nodded back. "Uh, Mackenzie I'll be right back."

"No, you won't, slut." Mackenzie smiled, standing to leave. She gave Joel a hug and a kiss on the cheek. "Go do your thing. I need to get home anyway. Thanks for the pep talk."

Joel hugged her. "Are you going to be OK?"

"Yeah, we will get past this. We always do," Mackenzie said. "Call me later, boo."

CHAPTER 10

In deep thought, Mackenzie drove along the interstate after leaving Joel at Blu Cantina. DJ Breezy's raspy voice cut into her calming old school music program to warn of a car accident caused by a high-speed police chase. He said that traffic was backed up for miles. Mackenzie was able to exit the highway before she was caught in the gridlock.

She headed toward the eateries and boutiques of Little Five Points to take an alternate route home. Her plan was thwarted since apparently everyone else had the same idea. The surface streets were a stalled cacophony of horn honking, road rage and stop-and-go stress. Mackenzie gave up. After making sure that all her children were where they should be, she turned on Jazmine Sullivan and settled in for the snail's paced commute.

Stopped at a red light, Mackenzie was admiring a red coat in a boutique window when she spotted a quaint French café called: Le

Cyne Noir's. She remembered Beverly raving that the place had the best desserts in town, so she whipped her car into the parking lot to give them a try. If anything, the stop would be a nice reprieve from the irritating traffic.

As soon as she entered the café, the pleasant aromas of fresh baked pastries and fresh brewed coffee saturated her senses. Nina Simone's, *Feeling Good,* played in the background. A whimsical mural of a sunny spring day in Paris, showcasing a pond of black swans covered the walls. It wasn't packed, but the patrons that were there were either transfixed by their laptops or chatting over coffee and sweets.

Mackenzie was checking out the tempting display of treats when an older gentleman with a heavy French accent welcomed her. He offered her a sample of a chocolate filled eclair that was so scrumptious, Mackenzie ordered a half dozen to take home to the kids. She didn't notice someone approach her from behind, taping her on the shoulder. She turned around, surprised, and a little thrilled to see Dr. Lang's handsome, smiling face.

"That good, huh?" he asked, pointing out the splotch of chocolate on her chin. He offered her a napkin as she pulled a mirror from her purse.

"This is nothing," she said, wiping her chin clean. "You should see how messy my face gets when I get a hold of a strawberry cheesecake. How are you, Dr. Lang?"

"Tell you what, how about you call me, Andre. I'll call you Mackenzie after office hours."

"OK, Andre."

"I'm fine. Can't complain, Mackenzie. And you? When we spoke earlier you were understandably stressed out."

Mackenzie pointed to her face. "Don't let this steel facade fool you. I'm still stressed out." She smiled sweetly. "But with three kids and a demanding job, stress is not a luxury for me. So, I guess I'll get over it soon."

Andre nodded. "How's Traci. I know she must be relieved to know that she's in the clear."

"She's probably still a little shook up over the whole ordeal, but she'll be back to her old self soon, I hope. She definitely knows that the situation could have turned out a lot differently," Mackenzie said, nodding appreciatively to the Frenchman as he handed her the neatly packaged baked goods.

"That's good to know." He paused and stared at the ceiling like a man in deep thought. "Mackenzie if you're not in a hurry I was just about to have a coffee. Why don't you join me? The carmel chia latte here is excellent. Much better than Starbucks." He smiled.

Mackenzie subtly glanced at the wall clock behind him. She had a couple of hours before Traci was supposed to be home. Since the traffic outside showed no signs of letting up anytime soon, having coffee with an attractive doctor was an easy choice to make.

"That would be nice."

"Cool. Hey, Ramón two of my usual please, buddy," Andre told the Frenchman who had been watching their exchange.

"Coming right up," Ramón replied.

"Did you want anything else?" Andre asked Mackenzie.

Mackenzie held up her pink box of treats. "No thanks, I'm good."

They sat at a table near the cozy fireplace. Moments later, Ramón brought over their drinks in colorful, oversized mugs.

"So where are you from, Mackenzie?" Andre asked, taking off his blazer. "I've been trying to place your accent."

"Accent? I thought I'd gotten rid of that a long time ago." Mackenzie smiled and stirred her drink. "But, I'm from Savannah, Georgia. What about you?"

"Tupelo, Mississippi originally, but mostly grew up Memphis."

"OK. I've been there a couple of times. No wonder you moved." Mackenzie teased.

Andre laughed. "What's wrong with Tupelo?"

"Nothing if you like living in the 60's."

"Hey, that's my hometown you're talking about."

"I'm kidding. Tupelo is a wonderful town. I've been meaning to get back there actually. One of my sorority sisters just had a baby."

"Oh, you're Greek? Let me guess." He snapped his fingers. "Delta, right?"

"That's right Delta Sigma Theta," Mackenzie said, forming the Delta pyramid with her hands. I pledged at Clark Atlanta."

"I knew it. I can always spot a Delta lady."

"What about you? Did you pledge?"

"I pledged Kappa at TSU."

"A Kappa man," Mackenzie said. "So, what brings you to Atlanta, Andre?"

"Change of scenery, I guess." He shrugged. "I've been here about two and a half years now. I have a place not too far from here in Kirkwood Park."

"Oh, OK. You and your wife?" Mackenzie asked.

Andre's gaze dropped as he stirred his coffee. He looked at Mackenzie, wondering how he could tell her that he'd come home three years ago to discover that his wife and daughter were missing. That the killer had placed their slaughtered bodies in their bed three days later. But, sensibility forbade him. That was a morbid tale best kept to himself, his therapist, and in his nightmares.

"My wife, Rene, died three years ago, along with my sixteen-year-old daughter, Zhuri, that I mentioned before, in a fire," Andre told Mackenzie instead, evoking his nightmare.

Mackenzie was dumbstruck. She felt that for the second time in the same day she had intruded in this man's private life, stirring up painful memories.

"My God. I'm so sorry to hear that, Andre. Please excuse my thoughtlessness."

"Hey, there's nothing to excuse. You didn't know. Besides, that's what my therapist is for, remember?"

"Still, I should know better. Especially since I know how hard it can be. Like I told you before my husband passed away."

"How did he die, Mackenzie? If you don't mind me asking."

"Cancer. Lymphoma. A little over three years ago, also. I'm just getting to where I can talk about it, you know?"

"Yeah, I know," Andre replied, raising his coffee cup. "Look at the two of us having a pity party complete with lattes. At least it's better than the bottles of vodka I used to inhale."

Mackenzie clanked her cup to his. "We're a pair, right?" she said, taking a sip of coffee. "You're right. This is so much better than Starbucks."

"Told you. So, have you spoken to Joel?" Andre asked, seeking some comic relief.

"Yes. I just left him actually. I told him you said hello."

"Good." He smiled. "You know, I think that Joel had a little crush on me."

"Yes, I know," Mackenzie chuckled. She was shocked that Andre would acknowledge that. "Does that bother you?"

"Not at all. I'm completely secure with my sexuality. Actually, one of my best friends from undergrad is gay. He's good people. He respected me and I respected him. He taught me that people are just people no matter their sexual orientation."

"I'm glad to hear you feel that way," Mackenzie said, recalling Keith's sentiment. "People are just people."

They talked and flirted. They laughed out loud and shared intimately. Completely entranced with one another, isolated in their own little corner of Paris. Mackenzie spoke of her idealistic childhood in Savannah, GA with her loving parents and overprotective older brother, Nathan. She loved seafood, and summers spent at the beach. A passion for journalism had been discovered while working as editor of her high school newspaper, so choosing it as her major at CAU was an easy decision. She shared with Andre the undying love she still felt for her late husband, Marlon. And her worries about properly raising her children now that she was doing it alone.

Andre recounted his childhood in Memphis. He told her that he was an only child, though he had lots of cousins to fill the void. The woman Andre called his mother, Lillian Lang, was really his grandmother. She had raised him since his father was a no-show and his mother had died during his birth. This was a major reason for his decision to pursue a career as an OB/GYN. His deceased wife had been his one true love. They met while he was in medical school at the University of Tennessee during a party at neighboring Fisk University where Rene attended. Their only child was born a couple of years after they were married. Sadly, he admitted that their deaths had crippled him and there were times when he didn't know if he could go on.

They didn't realize that over an hour had passed until a young couple entered the café, with playful banter. Obviously in love, the couple invoked memories in them both, reminding them of their quiet longing.

Andre noticed Mackenzie look at her watch. "Don't tell me your ready to leave so soon?" he asked.

"Not at all. But, motherly duty calls." She sighed. "I need to be at home when Traci arrives. She and I have a lot to discuss."

"I understand." He dropped two twenties on the table. "I'll walk you to your car."

Outside the air was chilly, and the sun was casting its last rays of vibrant orange light.

"I'm really glad that I ran into you, Andre," Mackenzie said, opening her car door.

"Me too. Actually, I was hoping to see you again. On purpose, this time."

"I'll have to run that by Joel first. But I'd like that, also. Very much so."

"Cool. I'll call you, Mackenzie."

"I'll be waiting. Good night." She waved goodbye to him as she backed away.

Andre took a moment to process all that had just that taken place between him and Mackenzie. The laughter they shared. The simple easy pleasure of her company. He started for his SUV allowing himself to feel something he hadn't felt in a long time: Hope.

His eyes lit up, the corners of his lips contorted into a wicked smirk. A wolf spotting a cornered a lamb. He pictured plunging a knife down Lang's throat; the blood that would gush from his mouth. He reached into his glove compartment for his fifth cigarette. Smoking quelled the fiery rage that consumed him each time that he saw Lang.

At first it had angered him that the police did not release the details of how Dana Bradford, or whatever the hell her name was, had been killed. She was supposed to be his special little calling card. A warning that the past was neither forgotten, nor forgiven.

He was pissed that his plan wasn't going as he had envisioned— deviating from a plan leads to mistakes. That stupid bitch giving Lang a fake name was one. It also didn't help that the police portrayed her murder as merely the work of some horny punk who couldn't keep his dick in his pants. But he was patient. A murder that gruesome would have those dumb-fucks scrambling to find out the who's, what's, and how's. Just like in Memphis.

In hindsight, he saw that as a good thing. Now, he could inflict more damage. Now there would be a second victim. A third. Hell, a fourth or fifth, if necessary. What did he care? They were simply a means to an end. The more of Lang's patients he killed, the bigger the fallout. His resolve was unwavering. He wanted that motherfucker to suffer. Down on his knees as he cried out to his god. Lang would beg for death when he found out that vengeance had followed him to Atlanta and was killing his patients in the exact same manner as his bitch and his brat. He needed to know that there was no escape.

He sat up alert when he saw Andre leaving the cafe talking with Mackenzie, whom he didn't recognize. He grabbed his binoculars from the passenger seat for a closer look. She was a looker. Lang was drooling all over her, hanging on to her every word.

Interesting. So, the good doctor still has a little life in him after all, he sneered, blowing out smoke. *No problem. I'm gonna cut it out of him soon enough.*

He snatched up his binoculars again when he saw Mackenzie back into the street. Choosing to follow her instead of Lang, he quickly started up his car. If Lang was that fascinated with this woman, he was sure as hell going to find out every fucking thing about her.

CHAPTER 11

Every time that Andre visited his therapist, he waited five or ten minutes before they started his session. As usual, she was on the phone talking to whomever about whatever, while she subconsciously adjusted her oversized tortoise shell glasses even if they weren't slipping.

Dr. Roslyn Lewis was a small brown woman of about sixty with a shrill voice and a comical appearance, there was nothing small or comical about her credentials. Among other things, she had earned a doctrine from Stanford University's famed school of psychology. She had published several bestselling books and Andre, along with the rest of the world, held her and the counsel she gave in high esteem.

Dr. Lewis looked up at him as if she were just noticing his presence for the first time. She held up an index finger mouthing, 'One more minute.'

Andre didn't mind. He had a couple of hours before he had to see another patient and he was still riding high from his encounters with Mackenzie.

"OK. We'll talk later, darling. Bye, Bye." Andre heard her say to whomever she was speaking to in her adopted upper-crust accent. It amused him to hear her speak since he knew that she was from humble beginnings in Chitlins & Greens, South Carolina.

She smiled at him. "Andre. My apologies for the delay. That was my agent on the phone. Can you believe that we are negotiating a television talk show?"

"That's fantastic. Look out Iyanla." He smiled. "Congratulations, Roslyn."

"Thank you, darling. How are you?"

"I'm doing really great," he said surprised that he used the word great to describe his emotional state.

"I can tell," she said, sitting back in her chair, clasping her tiny hands together in observation. "You're positively glowing."

"Thank you."

Roslyn stood, adjusted her pink skirt suit and made her way over to the sitting area of her office. She sat and then poured herself a steaming cup of tea. Andre followed, turning down her offer for tea.

"So, tell me, Andre. What is responsible for your ebullience? What has happened since last we spoke?" she asked, crossing her legs.

"I'm still adjusting to Atlanta. The new practice is going well."

"OK. That's great." She opened her leather binder to take notes.

"And I know that I probably shouldn't be feeling this excited this soon," Andre said cautiously. "But I met a woman, Dr. Lewis."

She smiled. "That's wonderful, darling. Tell me more."

"Well her name is Mackenzie. Her daughter is a patient of mine and her best friend was my interior designer. She and I ran into each other at a cafe near my place on Friday."

"That's nice. What happened?"

"It was probably unprofessional, but it just came over me to ask her to join me for a coffee. The next thing I knew, we were hitting it off like we had known each other for years. We had a great conversation before she had to leave, then we continued it when I called her Sunday afternoon. She's amazing, Dr. Lewis. I haven't felt this way in a long time. Truthfully, it's exciting...And maybe a little strange."

"Why do you feel that it's strange, Andre?" Dr. Lewis asked.

"I'm just surprised that I'm feeling this way about a woman. It's been a long time." Andre hesitated. "I lied to her, Dr. Lewis."

"Lied?"

"I told her that Rene and Zhuri died in a fire."

"Like in your dream." Dr. Lewis made notations in her binder. "And why did you lie?"

"I just didn't want to scare her off, I guess. I mean if you're just meeting someone how do you tell them that you came home to find your family slaughtered."

"I can't imagine." She sympathized. "Do you plan on telling her should your relationship advance beyond cafes and Sunday morning phone calls?"

"I hadn't thought that far ahead."

"You should think about it," Dr. Lewis said. "Visualizing yourself telling someone other than me about your past is an important part of your healing process, Andre."

"Yes." He sighed deeply. "I know. But this is all premature. We haven't even had an official date yet."

"Yes, darling. But the implications are not. The mere fact that you are feeling as you are feeling suggests to me that you are ready for the second phase of your life. An end to your solitary existence."

"Perhaps."

"Perhaps indeed," she said, taking a sip of tea. "So, tell me more about this angelic Mackenzie."

"Mackenzie Hill," Andre said with a twinkle in his eyes. "She's thirty-nine, an AP award winning journalist at the Atlanta Star. She's smart, beautiful, and very funny. She has three children. A fifteen-year-old daughter and six-year-old twin boys."

"An Associated Press award? Impressive. Is she divorced?"

"Widowed."

"Widowed? I see. A widow with a fifteen-year-old daughter. Interesting," Dr. Lewis said, jotting down more notes.

"Roslyn," Andre sighed. He could practically see the gears whirling in her head. He got up and walked over to the window. People down on the busy street were hustling to get out of the light rain. "Are you purposely trying to kill my good mood?"

"Of course not. It's my duty to get you to ask yourself these questions."

"I see where you're going with this, so I'm going to stop you right now. It's not what you think."

"And what am I thinking, Andre?" She challenged him.

He glanced back. "You think that I'm so excited about Mackenzie because I see her and her daughter as substitutes for Rene and Zhuri."

"Two people connecting over the shared loss of loved ones is very powerful. Any psychologist worth their degree would make that observation."

"Well, let me make myself clear," Andre said firmly, reseating himself. "There could never be a substitute for them. And I'm not looking for one."

"The subconscious is very powerful," Dr. Lewis replied. "You cannot tell me you don't see—"

He cut her off. "Roslyn, this is pointless. It's all just a coincidence."

"Don't take offense, darling." She smiled to defuse him. "This is why you pay me so handsomely."

Andre chuckled, realizing that he needed to cool down. "Is it too late to cancel that last check?"

———————

"Excuse me, ma'am. Is this the office of the backstabbing man stealer?" Mackenzie heard someone ask in a poorly disguised voice.

She didn't have to look up from her computer to know that Joel was leaning in her doorway.

"What are you doing here?" she replied without missing a keystroke.

He flopped down in one of the chairs in a front of her desk.

"Meeting a new client at those new lofts down the street, so you know that I couldn't resist coming by to get on your nerves a little. What are you up to?"

"Trying to meet my deadline for this story. What's another word for happiness?"

"Another word? Please. I still can't define the first one."

"You're useless."

"Yeah. Cute though. So, you better keep your new man from around me."

"Andre is hardly my man, Joel," she said, grinning slyly. Her cell phone chimed, announcing a new text message.

"I can't tell from the way you were going on and on about him on the phone last night and this morning. That's probably him texting you now," Joel replied, watching Mackenzie reply to the message.

"Actually, Mr. Know-it-all, this is from Traci checking in."

"Oh. Are things going well in the Hill house?"

"We're getting there," Mackenzie said slowly. "Traci and I have been having serious heart-to-hearts. She admits her mistakes. I admitted that I was taking her for granted, but I still had to punish her. That tight six-month restriction with no after school activities and checking in with me as soon as she gets home is the best I could come up with."

"What about, Antonio? Any word from him?"

"Well, his parents and I tried to come up with a solution, though realistically we know we can't really stop them from seeing each other. We only can hope that they will listen to what we've told them. Traci assured me that she is going to abstain, but I'm thinking about putting her on birth control."

"I'm sure you can believe her."

"I hope so."

So, tell me what's going on with you and the good doctor?"

"Honestly, I don't know," she said and paused from typing. "It's strange but I feel so drawn to him."

Joel laughed. "Yeah, Jezebel. I felt drawn to him, too. He's fine as hell. It's called lust."

"No. Not that. I mean he is fine. But there's a lot more to it than just his looks. He's a great guy, Joel. I like his humor, his intelligent, and his courage is inspiring."

"Courage?"

"Yeah. I thought that I told you that he lost his wife and daughter in a fire."

"No, you didn't. You only told me that he had a daughter. You never said anything about a wife or a fire."

"Well, he told me that it happened about three years ago in Memphis. Andre didn't say it, but I believe that's the reason that he moved here."

"Damn, that's depressing."

Mackenzie reached for her thesaurus. "Yeah, I know."

"When are you seeing him again?"

"Soon I hope. We made plans to get together this week but between the kids and deadlines, I don't see how."

"Child, please." Joel said with mocked urgency. "You better ship those kids over to my place. Hell, I'll even type up the damn articles for you. Anything to get you some action."

They both laughed.

"So, you never did tell me about that guy you ditched me for at Blu Cantina," Mackenzie said.

"First of all, I didn't ditch you. Stop being so dramatic. Secondly, nothing happened. We talked at the bar, had a couple more drinks, then went back to his place."

"And?"

"And nothing. He failed to mention that he had a live-in girlfriend and a son. There were pictures, toys, and run over high heels all over the place. That nigga whipped out his dick and said that we had to hurry up before they got home. I told him I left something in the car and got the hell out of there."

"Joel Sanders running out on men? What's the world coming too?"

"It's not that serious. I just realized that I'm tired of the same old bull. And I'm definitely not into down low guys anymore. The thrill was cute when I was younger, but they are way too much trouble."

With only a light tap on the door to announce herself, Jackie floated into Mackenzie's office on a cloud of aristocratic superiority and expensive perfume. Dominique Deveraux would have been proud. She started to address Mackenzie, pausing when she realized that Joel was in the room. In their usual manner, Jackie and Joel exchanged phony pleasantries while eying each other like two pit bulls. Mackenzie felt she would have to turn the hose on them at any moment.

"Is this a bad time?" Jackie asked Mackenzie.

"No, Jackie. Joel was just leaving," Mackenzie said in Joel's direction.

"I was?"

"Yes, you were," Mackenzie said through gritted teeth. "We'll continue our discussion later."

Joel stood to leave. "I'll call you later." Then to Jackie he smirked, "It was so good seeing you again, Jackie. And I love your outfit. Sears, right?"

Jackie dismissed his thinly veiled insult. She sat down with a peculiar expression on her face that Mackenzie couldn't decipher. The most she could tell was that Jackie was fretting over something.

"How can I help you?" Mackenzie asked her.

"Mackenzie, do you recall that day when you came into my office and I was crying?"

"Yes," Mackenzie answered slowly, surprised at Jackie's admission.

"I want to apologize for being a bitch that day."

What about all the other days? Mackenzie wondered to herself. "It's OK, Jackie. We all have our bad days."

"No, it's not OK," Jackie insisted. "You were trying to show genuine concern, and I behaved badly."

"Don't even worry, Jackie. It's long forgotten like water off a duck's back."

"Mackenzie, I didn't come in here just to apologize."

"OK. What's up?"

"I really need to talk to someone. Does your offer still stand?"

"Yes, of course. Are you OK Jackie?" Mackenzie noticed that Jackie was struggling to maintain her composure. She got up from her desk and sat next to her.

Jackie whispered, "Cancer."

"What do you mean?"

"They say that it's cancer in my breast." Jackie sobbed.

"Oh, Jackie," she said. Catching them both off guard, Mackenzie reached over to embrace her.

"I'm sorry to bother you with this Mackenzie. I know that you have your own problems. I just don't have anyone else."

Mackenzie offered Jackie a tissue to wipe her tears.

"I'm honored that you came to me. Now tell me, Jackie, are they sure?"

"Yes, my doctor says that the test indicates stage four malignancy."

Mackenzie squeezed Jackie's hand. "So what are you going to do now? Have you gotten a second opinion? When are you going to start treatment?" Mackenzie fired questions at Jackie as her mind flooded with memories of Marlon. The shock of the initial the diagnosis, the retest and the second opinion. Realizing that she was being insensitive, Mackenzie put her own pain aside to console Jackie.

"Um…" Jackie sniffed. "I've decided to go back home to Oakland to be near my only family, my cousin, and to clear my head while I get things in order. My oncologist referred me to a specialist out there, so I'll start treatments soon." Jackie lowered her head as she sobbed. "What keeps me up at night is knowing that my mother died of the same thing when she was my age."

"Well, whatever you need, whatever I can do, I'm here for you, Jackie," Mackenzie said, embracing her.

Jackie looked at Mackenzie. She didn't need to say anything. Mackenzie saw the gratefulness in her eyes that conveyed that no matter how their relationship had played out in the past, or however they would interact in the future, Mackenzie would never see Jackie as the unapproachable ice queen. Jacqueline Smalls was simply a terrified woman who had just learned the value of life and unconditional friendship.

CHAPTER 12

After leaving therapy, Andre took the scenic route to his office through Buckhead, admiring the tree lined streets and stately homes. The slow pace gave him time to think about what he and Dr. Lewis had discussed. As always, she had ended their session by reminding him to forgive himself. To stop wandering through life as if it were a nightmare he was hoping to wake from. To find life after death.

Andre questioned Dr. Lewis' evaluation. He truly believed that he had taken significant steps toward his healing. Besides he was no longer wearing his wedding ring and had started getting out of the house more. He purchased new clothes, and a few decorative items to brighten up his lifeless place. Even his nightmares had been less frequent. Still, if he were to be completely honest with himself, Andre understood exactly what Dr. Lewis meant. Outside of work, his life had little social contact. The only reason that he had bumped into Mackenzie was because she had fortuitously stumbled on part of his daily routine at Le Cyne Noir's.

Deep down he hoped his sudden epiphany had nothing to do with his meeting Mackenzie. He in no way wanted to give any credence to Dr. Lewis' inference that he saw Mackenzie along with Traci as convenient substitutes for the world he had lost.

Sooner than he would have liked Andre caught sight of his office plaza. Driving into the lot, he saw Paula's beat up beige Honda Civic parked next to Ciara's green Jetta. There was no reserved parking, but Andre's usual spot was occupied by a black vintage Charger. Paula's fiancé Chris' car. Andre dreaded the inevitable encounter with Chris. As hard as he tried Andre couldn't bring himself to like the man. There was something creepy and disingenuous about him.

Andre didn't see what a wholesome girl like Paula saw in him. As far as Andre could tell, Chris did not work and had latched on to Paula with all the determination of a starved leech. Andre parked in a spot amongst the patrons of the various professionals occupying the plaza. Just as he turned to grab his briefcase and jacket from the backseat, he spotted Chris exiting the office. He was counting a wad of cash that he had no doubt bummed off Paula. Andre decided to wait until Chris drove off so that he could avoid the phony conversation.

Damn, Andre grimaced when he realized that Chris saw him, smiling and waving as he walked toward Andre.

Chris had a walk that Andre would describe as a zombie lurch. He leaned forward in a way that kept his head one step ahead of his body, while using his long legs to lunge himself forward. Chris probably considered himself white, but it was obvious that he had other ethic influences not far down in his bloodline. Asian or possibly Native American as evident by his coloring, slanted eyes and well pronounced cheekbones.

Andre stepped out of his Range Rover and prepared himself for Chris' nonsensical discourse.

"Hey, Chris. How are you doing, man?" Andre dryly asked as he shook Chris' out

stretched hand. It was clammy as usual.

"Not too bad, Doc. Not too bad," he replied, still wildly shaking Andre's hand. "Just stopped by to bring Paula some lunch."

"Is that right?"

"Yep. Gotta take care of my lady, you know." Chris stepped back to have a good view of Andre's SUV. "Nice ride you got here doc," he whistled, peering inside. "Real nice. Must have set you back, what? Fifty, sixty grand?"

"Something like that."

"Yeah? It's a shame though. All this space and no family to fill it with. Rich single guy like you should be driving a Porsche or something. I have a friend that can get you a good deal if you're interested."

Blasé Andre replied, "I'll keep that in mind. Listen Chris it was good seeing you again, but if you'll excuse me I have patients to see."

"Don't let me keep you," he replied, raising his hands in false surrender. "Gotta take care of those pregnant ladies. You know what they say. The children are our future. I can't wait until me and Paula start poppin' them out. I want a sweet little baby girl first."

"Right," Andre said going around Chris toward his office. "See you around."

He had only gotten a few feet away when he heard Chris call out, "Doc."

Andre was annoyed. "Yes, Chris?" he sighed, looking back.

"Don't forget about my friend," he winked.

"Excuse me? What friend?"

"The guy who can get a single guy like you into a Porsche."

"Oh. I won't," Andre said, his skin crawling as he resumed his path. There was no question. He definitely did not like Christian Terry.

_____

Leaving her office for home Mackenzie was glad that she was the only one in the elevator as it descended toward the parking garage. She welcomed the solitude from the rest of the world, even if it were just for a fleeting moment. Jackie's revelation about having breast cancer had her eyes glistening with memories from Marlon's ordeal.

The cancer has spread to most of his organs, Mackenzie heard the haunting voice of one doctor repeat in her mind. *Chemo or radiation therapy would probably not be effective at this point…They would only make matters worse by adding unnecessary pain and suffering to the inevitable.*

The doctors had given Marlon only six months to live.

"Six months," Mackenzie whispered, clutching her briefcase against her chest.

She and Marlon had refused to give up. Marlon promptly resigned his position as a senior research microbiologist at the CDC. In desperation, he and Mackenzie sought out specialist after specialist for someone that offered hope in saving his life. All the doctors gave the same bleak prognosis: Death.

In the end, Marlon decided to try chemotherapy. Mackenzie was forced to watch the handsome, robust, charismatic man that she loved so dearly wither away to a shell that she barely recognized. She closed her eyes and said a silent prayer for Jackie. No one should have to go through what Marlon went through.

Without her paying attention, the elevator stopped at the sixteenth floor. One person got on but Mackenzie was too lost in bad memories to notice that it was her, Keith.

"Mackenzie, are you OK?" he asked, noticing her wipe away tears.

Mackenzie came out of her trance. "Oh. Hey, Keith. Yeah, I'm OK," she slowly said. "A friend just gave me some bad news." She squared her shoulders to feign composure. "Long time no see. How have you been?"

"Been OK. Still working hard on these cases. Matter fact, I was just on the sixteenth floor questioning a potential witness for the Walter's trial."

"Oh, really. Any new developments?"

"No. Dead end."

"The jury is still in deliberation, right?"

"Yes, for the past two days," he replied as if the trial was wearing him thin and he wasn't expecting a positive outcome. "I'm really praying that we can get justice for the victim and her family, but since the judge tossed out some key evidence it's looking as if the verdict could go either way." Keith looked at Mackenzie. He could tell that whatever news that she had been given was weighing heavy on her. "Mackenzie, are you sure that you're OK?"

"I really appreciate your concern but I'm fine," she said. The elevator dinged to announce their arrival at parking level three. "This is my stop. It was good seeing you again, Keith. I guess I'll see you at the courthouse when the jury has a verdict."

"See you there." Keith smiled as the door closed in front of him. He rode the elevator down to the next level and got out to wait around for a few minutes. His car was parked on the same level where Mackenzie had gotten off, but he sensed that she needed to be alone. He never wanted to force himself on her, which is why he resisted the urge to call her more than the one time he did after their disappointing date.

Seeing her try to put on a brave front had moved him. He wanted to take Mackenzie in his arms. Let her know that he would always be there. Give her the moon and right any wrongs in her life. He pressed the UP button. As he stepped through the elevator doors Keith had an epiphany: He was in love with Mackenzie Hill.

CHAPTER 13

Laughter came from Mackenzie's room as she talked to Joel via Facetime. He had called to offer a little encouragement about her date with Andre and to throw in his two cents about what Mackenzie was wearing.

"Your haircut looks cute," Joel said. "Let me see the back."

Mackenzie posed in the camera to show off her new layered bob cut. "Do you approve?"

"I do. It freshens you up. About time you got rid of that outdated length." Joel said. "Now let me see what you are wearing?"

She held up a black halter gown to her chest. "This with black heels and those emerald teardrop earrings you gave me last year."

"Chic," Joel said. "I taught you well."

The house phone rang. It was her mother.

"Call you later," she said, putting the phone on speaker.

"Hey, mama. Where's daddy?" Mackenzie asked, sliding into her dress.

"I don't know," her mother replied a little too impersonally. "Off with his golfing buddies or something, I guess. So, tell me, baby. What's this I hear about this handsome doctor you've been seeing? A little bird told me that things are getting serious."

"A little bird, huh? And who might that be?" Mackenzie rolled her eyes knowing that the little bird with the big mouth was no one but, Beverly. She could picture them on the phone cackling like two barn yard hens about her love life and was instantly sorry she had ever confided in Beverly.

"That's not important. What is important is that you didn't bother to tell me anything. So, who is he? He sounds like the cat's meow from what I hear."

Mackenzie sighed, knowing that her mother would persist until she knew everything about Andre, right down to the size of his underwear. "His name is Andre, mama. He's a doctor. We only just met so I'd hardly call things serious. Right now, we are just two people getting to know one another. And yes, he actually is a great guy."

"Is that right?" her mother said. She was excited. "Well, take your time, baby. Don't scare him off. I just get so worried about you sitting alone in that big house with all those sad memories."

I could say the same thing about you. "I'm not alone, mama. The kids are here. Please don't worry about me. I'm fine."

"I know you are, baby," Mrs. Gwendolyn Jones said. "Is he a good Christian man? The marrying kind?"

"Marriage? Mama, that's the last thing on either of our minds. It's not nearly that serious, so you might want to stop listening to that little bird of yours."

"Well, you should start thinking about it, Mackenzie. I know you're still hurting over Marlon. He was a fine man, but Lord only knows what I would have done without your father."

Mackenzie had heard enough. She was not about to let her mother spoil her night before it had even begun. Still, she made sure to keep her tone respectable.

"Well, right now we're just two people enjoying each other's company. If something more develops, I'll make sure that you are the first to know. As a matter of fact, Andre's on his way to take me out, so I'll call you tomorrow. Bye mama. Love you."

The doorbell chimed throughout the house.

"I'll get it," Mackenzie heard Traci yell.

Andre stood on the stoop of Mackenzie's home. He heard someone approach and gave his tuxedo a quick once-over. Without him noticing, the door opened, and Traci caught him bent over wiping a scuff from his shoes.

"I don't think that my mom will notice that tiny spot," Traci teased him.

Andre stood upright smiling. "How are you, Traci?"

"I'm OK," she replied. "Turn around, let me get a good look at you."

A good sport, Andre did as he was asked. "So, do I pass?"

"Yeah, you look real nice. Come on in." He followed her through the foyer to the living room. "You can have a seat. I'll go get my mom, Dr. Lang."

"Thanks." He sat on the sofa. Before long, she came down the stairs.

"Hey, Andre. Sorry to keep you waiting," Mackenzie said as Andre stood to greet her. "I was getting the twins settled."

"I don't mind at all," he said. He gave her a hug. "You look stunning."

"Thank you. You clean up nice, too."

"Thanks, Mackenzie."

"Too bad your shoes are all scuffed up," she added with a straight face. Mackenzie's poker face broke down when Andre's eyes dropped to his feet. "I'm joking. Traci asked me to mess with you about that."

Andre laughed, taking Mackenzie's arm in his. "Well please allow me to escort you to dinner pretty lady. Scuffed shoes and all."

Mackenzie and Andre arrived at Orbit atop a glass, cylindrical hotel towering above downtown Atlanta. Firefly-esque lights floated in midair, adding a touch of magic to the low-lit restaurant. Slowly rotating, it treated patrons to spectacular views of the glittering southern metropolis seventy-two stories below. The Hope Charity Ball was packed for pediatric healthcare. An opportunity to dress up and schmooze with the who's who of Atlanta didn't hurt either.

Andre and Mackenzie had enjoyed a decadent three-course meal, live music, and great conversation. Their enjoyable evening was interrupted by a middle-aged man with wrinkled sun, damaged skin and obvious hair plugs.

"Dr. Lang, how are you?" Hair Plug said with a wild handshake.

"Dr. Mitzner," Andre half-smiled. "I'm well. Just here doing our part for the cause. And yourself?"

"Pretty fantastic." He grinned. "And who is this lovely young lady?"

Andre introduced him to Mackenzie. "Mackenzie this is Dr. George Mitzner."

"Nice to meet you," they both said.

"This is my fiancé. My muse. Brandy," George said, wrapping his arm around the young trophy blonde who had materialized next to him. She handed him a glass of dark liquor. "Thank you, honey," he said to her.

Mackenzie and Andre glanced at each other, trying not to laugh as they exchanged greetings with the preteen who surely out past her curfew. "Well, good seeing you, George. Nice meeting you Brandy." Andre said, taking Mackenzie by the hand to make their escape.

"Lang," George said, grabbing Andre by the arm. "If you have a moment I wanted to talk to you again."

"Actually, George, I—"

George interrupted before Andre could decline. "This will only take a minute. And Brandy can keep Mackenzie company while you and I talk."

Mackenzie watched him dragged Andre away. Andre mouthed, "be right back" to her. She looked over at Brandy. Her knee length pink bandage dress constricted her circulation. "So, are you enjoying the ball?"

"Hell no." Brandy rolled her eyes. "I wanted to go to that hot new restaurant in Buckhead, but he dragged me here." Every other word she said sounded like she was asking a question.

Mackenzie tried to be cordial. "Don't you appreciate the cause? The foundation will help a lot of children."

Brandy scoffed while looking around in disgust. "Yeah, I guess. It's just so boring."

Mackenzie smiled politely and continued sipping the last of her champagne.

"So, your man's hot," Brandy said, out of the blue. She leaned in to whisper as if she were sharing a dirty secret. "Black guys have huge cocks, right?"

Thoroughly offended, Mackenzie leered at her ignorance. "Excuse me," she said. "I think I see one of my friends over there. Nice meeting you, Brandy." She saw Andre and George having what seemed to be an intense conversation. Not wanting to disturb them, she helped herself to another glass of champagne from a passing waiter. Mingling with anyone other than Brandy was a much better option. She was looking down at the twinkling cityscape when Andre wrapped his arms around her from behind.

"Where's your date?" he whispered in her ear.

"I'm not sure," she said, without turning around. "The last I saw him he ran off and left me with a crazy girl."

"He must be a fool to leave a beautiful woman like you alone."

"I'm still trying to figure that out."

Andre spun her around, drawing her close to him by her waist. "Well, he's a lame dude who doesn't deserve you. Let's get out of here. Go to my place. I'll show you a better time."

———————

Andre lived in a charming bungalow in the historic Kirkwood Park neighborhood, not far from the cafe where they had first run into one another. He was playing around on the porch with Mackenzie when his neighbor came rushing out of her house next door. She was an ebony-skinned older woman, wearing a turquoise tracksuit. Clearly upset about something, she looked the part of a worried grandmother who had been waiting up all night for her beloved grandson.

She could barely get her words out fast enough. "Dr. Lang, I was waiting," she gasped, stopping in mid-sentence when she noticed Mackenzie. "Oh, hello young lady. Excuse me, doctor. I didn't expect you to have company."

"It's OK, Mrs. Russell," he said. "This is my friend, Mackenzie Hill."

"Nice to meet you," Mackenzie said.

"Likewise," Mrs. Russell replied, seeming to have forgotten all about whatever had her so agitated. "It's good to see Andre out for a change. You two look so nice together."

"Thank you," Mackenzie said.

"Mrs. Russell. What were you saying before?" Andre asked.

Mrs. Russell reverted to her flustered state with ease. "Oh, yes. I was waiting to tell you that there was someone prowling around your place tonight. I saw him when I was out for my evening walk. I think he saw me, too. I called the police, but, of course, he was long gone before those slow pokes showed up."

"Were you able to give them a description?" Andre asked.

"No. I didn't see him very well, but I just wanted to let you know keep an eye out for any suspicious characters lurking around."

"You too. Thank you, Mrs. Russell," Andre said.

"You're welcome. We have to look out for each other. There's a lot of crazy people out here," she said, heading back to her house. "Nice meeting you, Mackenzie."

"You too, Mrs. Russell." Mackenzie waved. "Good night." Mackenzie turned to Andre. "She's sweet."

"Yeah, she is," Andre said.

As soon as Andre opened the door, his mini cocker spaniel met them, yapping as she bypassed Andre to head straight for Mackenzie.

"She's so cute," Mackenzie said, kneeling. The dog lay on her back, anticipating Mackenzie's belly rub. "That's a good girl." She turned to Andre. "Lilly, right? Named after your grandmother, Lillian."

Andre nodded. "Yeap. My ole take a switch to your butt, then fix you a plate of good home cookin', Granny," he said, smiling. "You can make yourself at home, while I let her outside. Come on, girl." Lilly followed him as he opened the French doors to the backyard.

Mackenzie took a seat on Andre's comfortable tan leather sectional. "She goes outside by herself?"

"Yeah," he said, heading to the kitchen. "She's a good girl. She'll take care of her business then come right back." Andre held up two bottles of wine. "I've got some cheap red or even cheaper white."

Mackenzie chuckled. "Nothing like a good cheap red."

"Coming up."

Feeling good, Mackenzie took her shoes off and put her feet up on the sofa. A little presumptuous, but she had a feeling that he wouldn't mind. She noticed his place. Like him, it was neat and orderly. Typically male in that there was probably little attention given to the minimalist décor. Lilly scurried back into the apartment and with one leap landed on Mackenzie's lap.

"Lilly, get down, crazy girl." Andre ordered from the kitchen.

"She's OK," Mackenzie said, rubbing Lilly's head softly.

Andre came back into the living room carrying two glasses of wine and a bowl of strawberries. He sat one glass and the bowl on the coffee table then shooed Lilly away. She ran off with one of her squeaky toys.

"Here you are," he said, offering Mackenzie the other glass. "I'll be right back. Let me change out of this penguin suit."

"OK."

When Andre left the room Mackenzie noticed a large framed picture leaning on the mantel. She went over for a closer look. It was of a woman and a pre-teen girl that must have been Andre's wife and daughter. Small white candles were placed in a neat semicircle around the photo.

The two of them were standing in front of the Egyptian pyramids. Andre's wife was an earthy beauty with long braids, and big infectious eyes that invited comparisons with Dorothy Dandridge.

Andre's cheesing daughter was his spitting image, framed by braids like her mother's, with his creamy coloring and bright smile.

"Such a tragedy," Mackenzie whispered to Lilly who was sitting on the floor next to her.

"That was taken about four years ago in Giza," Andre said from behind.

"Very lovely," Mackenzie said, turning to face him. Andre had removed his shirt and tie and was now wearing a white tank top exposing the lean fit body of a man half his age.

"Yes, they are," Andre said, raising the photo. "Zhuri, had made honor roll again in school that year. Rene and I told her we could do anything she wanted to do that summer. Ever since she saw the Pyramid Coliseum in Memphis, she was always fascinated by ancient Egypt, so that was her choice to see the real pyramids up close. Can you believe it? Not Disney World, or a beach trip like other kids her age. She wanted to go to Egypt."

"You must have been very proud."

"I was proud." He wiped a smudge off the glass. "I still am." He sat it back its place and gently took Mackenzie by the hand. "Come sit with me."

They relaxed on the sofa. Andre instructed his virtual assistant, to dim the lights, and to set the music mood. To add to the ambience, he lit several orange, ginger-peach scented candles that were on his glass coffee table. Classic R & B music filled the room. He put his legs up on the sofa. Mackenzie slid between his thighs, resting the back of her head against his chest.

"Mmm, this is nice," Mackenzie moaned, taking in the seductive sounds of the music, the stimulating taste of the wine, mixed with the sensual scents coming from both the candles and Andre. "The perfect cap to a perfect night. Thanks for inviting me."

"No problem. Thanks for coming with me. I don't think I could have handled those annoying people alone," he said, taking a sip of wine.

"I know exactly how you feel. When go to media events I always make sure that I know where the exits are in case I have to make an escape." Mackenzie chuckled. "At least the gala was for a good cause."

"True."

"I meant to ask. What's the deal with that doctor with the trophy girlfriend that pulled you away?"

"Dr. Mitzner? He keeps pressing me to join his practice."

"Ok. Is that something that you'd consider?

Andre paused. "I'm happy with my little practice," he shrugged. "Besides, they perform abortions and I choose not to"

Mackenzie looked up at him. "Does it go against your religious beliefs?"

Andre paused. "Not really. Just personal reasons," he said. "Close your eyes for me."

Mackenzie did as he asked. Andre sensuously slid a sweet strawberry across her lips before feeding it to her. Mackenzie did the same to him. Their seductive feeding led to deep kissing. Both loved the intimacy.

He leaned in for more kissing, sending long forgotten sensations racing through her body. She was breathless and yearning for more when Andre pulled his lips away.

Mackenzie rose to straddle him. with no intentions of stopping what they had started. His full lips worked overtime from her mouth to neck, while his strong hands caressed her breast and cupped her soft ass. Mackenzie threw her head back, moaning softly. The smoldering heat of sexual desire increased between her legs when Andre's substantial manhood pressed against her inner thighs.

In tuned to her body's calling, Andre unzipped her dress then gently lay her on the sofa.

"Andre," she whimpered, arching her back. He relived her of her bra, mouthing her breast, which had been tucked away and neglected for far too long. Mackenzie's body tingled at every spot Andre's mouth and hands touched. Eager to return the favor, she couldn't get his T-shirt off fast enough to begin licking his defined chest and chiseled abs.

"Mackenzie," Andre whispered as she moved to undo his trousers, intent on releasing his erection. "Are you sure that you're ready for this?"

She paused, then lay on her back in anticipation of what would come next. "Yes," she said. "I'm ready."

He stripped her of her remaining garments to give her what she wanted—what they both needed. Then it happened. When songstress, Anita Baker, sang the first verse of gratitude for love in her song, *Giving You the Best That I've Got*, Andre instantly knew that he had chosen the wrong playlist. Like one of Pavlov's dogs, conditioned to respond to a specific sound, the sexual fire that had burned within him seconds earlier was now cold. Anita sang,

"We love so strong and so unselfishly.
And I tell you now.
That I made a vow.
I'm giving you the best that I got…"

Andre's recalled a moment of intimacy between him and Rene years earlier.

One rainy Sunday morning while he slept, Rene had crawled back into bed serenading that song in his ear. Their wedding song. Lords knows that she couldn't sing, but at that moment there could not have been a sweeter sound on Earth. It was also the song he played endlessly after she had been killed. In a flash, the sweet memory was swapped with horrific images of Rene and Zhuri lying butchered in their bed.

Sensing that something wasn't right, Mackenzie sat up on her elbows. She noticed that his promising erection was now limp.

"Andre, is something wrong?"

Her eyes flickered in candlelight. Her curvaceous body gave no clue that she had mothered three children. Any man would love to be where he was right now. Instead, she chose to be with a sorry excuse for a man who was hindered by a song.

"Mackenzie, I really think we should wait for this," he said.

"What do you mean?" she asked. "Did I do something wrong?"

"No. No. It's not you," he said, taking her by the hand. "It's me. I'm really not ready."

"What? It's not you it's me?" She snatched her hand away and grabbed her dress from the floor to cover herself. "Oh, my God. I'm so embarrassed. Was I moving, too fast?"

"No, you weren't at all and you have no reason to be embarrassed. I—"

She cut him off. "Andre, I think that you should take me home."

"Mackenzie, don't be like that," he pleaded. "I want you to stay. Let's talk about this."

Her eyes welled up with tears. "I just think that I'll be more comfortable in my own home tonight."

Andre sighed. "OK. If that's what you want, I'll take you."

"Thank you," she said. "Where's your bathroom. I need to get myself together."

He directed her down the hall, to the second door on the right. Mackenzie grabbed her clothes and shoes. She scampered away, taking her bruised pride along with her.

Andre put his t-shirt on and sat on the sofa. *What was he doing? Why couldn't he get pass this?* It seemed as if he was never going to be able to have a normal life or a healthy romantic relationship. What's more, Mackenzie certainly didn't deserve to be caught up in his problems.

"Damn," he whispered, slamming his fist on the sofa arm. "I've got to get control." The virtual assistant mistook his mumbling for commands. It started playing *Control* by Janet Jackson. Andre knocked it off the end table to the floor. "Shut up."

After a few minutes, Mackenzie reentered the living room with her clothes back on. If she had seen or heard his outburst she made no mention of it. When Andre tried to make eye contact with her, hoping that his eyes would convey his sincere apology, Mackenzie only looked away.

"I'm ready," was all that she said.

CHAPTER 14

"And he switched off just like that?" Joel asked Mackenzie, sitting on her kitchen counter top.

"Yeah, just like that," Mackenzie said, shrugging and was barely audible. "He said that he wasn't ready."

"Wow," Joel said. He reached for a wine glass hanging under the cabinet, then went over to the fridge.

Joel looked silly in an oversized red, bronze and white Atlanta Gladiators hockey jersey, watching Mackenzie prepare dinner. He had just spent the last ten minutes trying to convince her to go to a hockey game with him. Who would have guessed that a black, gay, interior designer enjoyed hockey? What made more sense was that Joel just didn't want to waste two tickets originally meant for him and some date that didn't materialize for whatever reason.

Mackenzie sighed. "Wow is right."

"Are you sure that you washed your cat good before you went out?" Joel asked, looking inside for a bottle of Chardonnay. "Maybe,

Andre, caught a whiff of something not too pleasant. Uh, where's your wine?"

Mackenzie stopped chopping her mushrooms. "See, this is why I don't like telling you things sometimes," she said, waving the knife. "That's not funny, Joel."

"Whoa. I'm only joking. Don't cut me, Lorena Bobbitt," he said, laughing over his shoulder. "Just trying to make you lighten up. I'm sure that his change of mind has nothing to do with you. Didn't you tell me that Andre was still coping with the death of his wife and child? That's some deep shit. The good doctor has obviously got some issues you don't easily get over. You of all people know that." Joel peered around the open refrigerator door munching on a piece of cheese. "And the wine is where?"

"Yeah, you're right," Mackenzie conceded. "Maybe, I'm being selfish and insensitive. Lord knows that I'm probably only a tiny bit more at peace than Andre. At least I got to say goodbye to Marlon before he died."

"See. You nailed it. You're a selfish, insensitive, bitch," he said, laughing and tapping the empty wine glass. "Wine please."

Mackenzie handed him the corkscrew from the drawer. "It's in the freezer. Pour me a glass too," she said. "One thing's for sure, you wouldn't be able to recognize me from the way that I was acting last night. You should have seen me, Joel. Maybe I had too much to drink at the gala, but I was throwing myself all over him then he went ice cold. I felt like such a fool."

"Throwing yourself?" Joel said, uncorking the bottle and pouring them a glass. "Not Mrs. Prim and Proper," he said, making air quotes. "See I told you that you were a Jezebel."

A car horned signified that Nate was dropping the twins home from football practice. They boys burst straight into the kitchen clad in their football uniforms, they reeked of grass and six-year-old sweat.

"Hey, mom. Hey, uncle Joel," they said, plowing to the fridge for a Gatorade.

"What's up, little dudes?" Joel beamed, giving them fist bumps. "Look at you two. You get bigger every time I see you. Pretty soon you'll both be as tall as me."

"Hey, babies. How was practice?" Mackenzie asked.

"Great." Rashad answered for them because Antwan was too busy swallowing as much drink as he could in one gulp. "We're gonna win tomorrow."

"Are you gonna come see us play, Uncle Joel?" Antwan asked after finally succeeding in quenching his thirst.

"Awww. Sorry little man, I can't. Uncle Joel has to work all day with an evil, ole woman who can't make her mind up about the color bathroom tiles she wants."

Mackenzie laughed. "Dinner will be ready in a little bit, boys. Go shower before we eat." The twins ran off shouting football tackling noises. "Make sure you put those dirty uniforms in the hamper." she yelled to them.

"They're going to be a couple of heartbreakers," Joel said.

"Of course. My children are the most beautiful children to have ever walked the earth." Mackenzie bragged.

"You must not have seen my baby pictures," he chuckled. "So anyway. Back to Dr. Andre *Fine Ass* Lang."

Mackenzie took a sip of wine as she stirred the simmering pot of spaghetti sauce.

"Yes?" she said coyly.

"So, what's going to happen now? You plan on seeing him again, right?" Joel rolled his eyes. "Please don't tell me that this is going to end up like you and whatshisface? That cop. 'Cause this will be two for two and still no action."

"Keith? No. Andre left a message saying how sorry he was and that he hoped to see me again. I haven't called him back just, yet. But I will. I really like him, Joel. I'm tempted to see what can happen between the two of us. I just don't plan on jumping his bones like that again." Mackenzie shook her head in disbelief. "I was so embarrassed."

"Don't be. I would have done the same thing."

"True, but you're a slut," Mackenzie pointed out.

Joel clanked his wine glass to hers. "See, that's why I love you so much. You know me so well."

———————

Alone in a corner of the gym, Andre punished a heavy boxing bag with a flurry of power punches that would have given Mike Tyson pause. Every breath left him with a hard grunt. He welcomed the pain trickling through his gloves. Beads of sweat running down his face. His tank top soaking wet. He ignored his fatigued body's screams for him to stop. He didn't want to. Anger about his pathetic actions last night and the way he had humiliated Mackenzie was his fuel.

Seeing Andre work the bag, a chubby guy who Andre had often seen doing more talking than working out came up to him.

"Whoa. Lookin' good, bro." He nodded. "You do any amateur boxing?"

Andre came out of his trance. "Thanks, man," he said, taking a swig from his water bottle. He pulled up his tank top to wipe the sweat from his forehead. "I trained some when I was in college. Now I do it just for the exercise."

"Cool. You got some skills, but I noticed your feet weren't grounded. You gotta plant those feet when you punch to get more balance, power, and control. Like this," he said, forming a stance that Andre paid little attention. It was curious to him how the people who needed to work on their own bodies had the most knowledge to give.

"Thanks, man," Andre smiled politely. "I'll try to remember that." Chubby walked away satisfied that he had schooled someone else on proper techniques.

Andre emptied the last bit of water from the bottle and headed to the juice bar to buy another. On the way, an attractive woman did her best to show off her well-toned body, while doing some suggestive stretches. She was probably used to men chasing her, but Andre had his sights set only on Mackenzie. He hoped to God that he didn't scare her away. There was so much potential for great things between them.

At the counter, he decided to get a green power smoothie and leave the gym instead. He pulled his debit card from his wallet and came across a business card from Dr. Lewis, his therapist. He had thought about calling her to discuss his actions last night but decided against it. He knew exactly where his problems stemmed from. It was time he applied the previous tools she had given him and deal with his demons without a psychological net.

On the way to his SUV he checked his phone again, hoping that Mackenzie had returned his messages. Still nothing. *No problem*, Andre thought driving out of the parking lot. *I'll just call her back. I'm not about to give up that easily.* The phone rang as Andre was merging into traffic.

"Hello," he answered, hoping that the unidentified number was Mackenzie.

The voice of a young girl said, "Daddy, when are you coming home? Me and mom miss you."

Andre almost swerved into the next lane. Thank goodness, the Sunday traffic was light.

"Excuse, me? Who is this?"

"Daddy this is your little girl," she continued.

"Who is this?" Andre demanded.

"This is Natasha, daddy."

"Natasha, you have the wrong number."

"Is this Richard Kelly?" the girl asked.

"No, it isn't," Andre quickly said. "You have the wrong number."

"I'm sorry," she giggled. "You sound just like my father."

"No problem," Andre said as the girl hung up. He sighed.

This was ridiculous. He shouldn't be getting this upset over a simple wrong number. The phone rang, again. Andre answered immediately seeing that it was his best friend, Ethan, calling from Houston.

"Brother," Andre answered.

"What's up, man," Ethan said.

"Just the person I need to talk too."

As far as courtrooms, Judge Ernestine Anderson ran hers like a tight ship. Among other pet peeves, she did not enjoy the media having access to her courtroom during a major trial. She set aside a small section for the storm surrounding the murder trial of Thomas Walters. Resolute. Most of the press was camped out in the hallways waiting on the impending verdict.

In a suit, dark as his mood, Keith sat next to the parents of the victim, Mr. and Mrs. Frank Stewart. The working-class couple held hands. Mrs. Stewart silently wept, her head resting on her husband's shoulder. Thomas' silver haired father, Randolph Walters, sat directly behind his son and his high-priced lawyers. At the adjacent table, the stoic prosecutor sat next to her assistant with her arms folded. They anxiously waited for the jury to re-enter the room. The trial had been an exhausting battle with each side garnering victories and no clear winner in sight.

The jury room door opened. Seven white men, three white women, one black women, and one black man who made up the jury shuffled into the jury box. The prosecutor became alert and Keith said a silent prayer to whomever was listening.

"Ladies and gentlemen of the jury, in the matter of the State of Georgia vs. Thomas Randolph Walters have you reached a verdict?" Judge Anderson asked.

The foreman, a dangerously underweight woman, stood and cleared her throat. "Yes, we have," she squeaked, holding up a manila folder paper.

Judge Anderson instructed her bailiff to bring the folder to the bench. Stone-faced so as not to give away the verdict, she silently read it then handed it back to the bailiff to return to the forewoman.

"All rise," the judge ordered. Thomas and his lawyers stood as well as the prosecution. "Mrs. Clayton."

Mrs. Clayton, the forewoman, began reading the verdict. "Superior Court of Georgia, County of Fulton. In the matter of the people of the of the State of Georgia vs Thomas Randolph Walters, case number D084569-9. On count of one cruelty to children, we the jury find the defendant, Thomas Randolph Walters, not guilty. On count two kidnapping in the first degree, we find the defendant not guilty. On count three, rape in the first degree, we find the defendant not guilty. On count four, the murder in the first degree of Kendra Lakiesha Stewart, we find the defendant, not guilty."

Every *not guilty* the forewoman said sent a shudder through Keith. He watched in disbelief as Mrs. Stewart fainted. Mr. Stewart stood up to loudly protest the injustices that he and his wife had suffered. An ecstatic Thomas Walters cheesed as he shook the hands of his grinning lawyers, then turned to embrace his father.

Keith couldn't understand how this could happen. Any reasonable person could see that Thomas Walters was clearly guilty.

Judge Anderson pounded her gamble to regain order in her courtroom. "So, say one, so say you all?" she asked the forewoman.

The forewoman took a quick poll of the jurors to confirm the unanimous verdict. "Yes," she said.

"Then thank you for your service. You are dismissed. As is the defendant. Case dismissed," Judge Anderson said with a final pound of her gavel.

Keith tried to help Mr. Stewart with his wife but he was shunned. "I'm so sorry," he said to them.

Outside, the bright sun seemed out of place in the sky as Keith lead the Stewarts down the steep stairs of the courthouse amidst the swarming reporters.

Thanks to their private bodyguards, Thomas, his father, and their entourage navigated through the frenzy. Thomas proclaimed to the microphones being shoved in his face how good it felt to be vindicated. He promised to give a statement later that evening at his family's Buckhead estate. A black Cadillac Escalade pulled up to whisked them away.

Keith was now joined by Parnell. They did their best to protect the Stewarts from the relentless press. Mr. Stewart held his arm around his wife as he bellowed that they did not wish to give any statements. Activist filled the streets with signs and loud chants of— No Justice! No Peace!—to protest the verdict. Riot police managed the angry crowd.

Just as Keith was helping Mrs. Stewart into the passenger seat of her car she suddenly turned to the crowd.

"That monster killed my baby," she cried out. "He killed her, and they let him go. Somebody, please tell me why they let him go." Her husband quickly came to her aid to calm her. He helped her into their Ford Taurus and sped away without looking back.

With the Stewarts out of the picture, the reporters turned their attention to Keith. He only gave them the standard, "No comment" as he and Parnell forged a path toward Keith's car. Keith tried to block out the questions being shouted at him.

He heard one female voice penetrate through the commotion: "Detective Wilson. How do you feel about Thomas Walters being acquitted here today?"

Keith froze in his tracks. He spun around to confront the ignorant reporter. It was Mackenzie. "How the fuck do you think I feel? I feel like shit." Chagrin, Keith didn't say anything further to her or offer any apologies. He simply turned to continue to his car.

"Wasn't that Mackenzie?" Parnell asked.

"Yeah," Keith said with a heavy sigh. "You know what, man? I can't do this shit no more. I quit."

CHAPTER 15

With Nate and Beverly to her left, Traci to her right, and her niece Ayana bouncing on her lap, Mackenzie sat in the bleachers of the DeKalb Memorial Stadium, cheering on the twins and her nephews. Excitement resonated throughout the stadium on the cool evening. Their team, the Oakwood Academy Eagles, sought to defeat their arch rivals, the Winston Country Day Bulldogs, in the playoff rounds of the Peewee Football League.

Mackenzie was attempting to both keep her eyes on the game and watch out for Andre. He had called earlier to see how Mackenzie was doing after the other night and to see if she wanted to get together. She had invited him to the game. The fact that it was now well into the last quarter, coupled with Andre's obvious hang-ups made Mackenzie doubt that he was going to show. Giving up on him and concentrating on her family seemed more sensible.

"Mackenzie. Is that him?" Beverly asked for the millionth time, pointing at yet another man that vaguely matched Mackenzie's description of Andre. When Mackenzie had told everyone that he would be joining them, Beverly ran with it. She even went so far as to announce her plans to invite him over for one of her overdone family dinners, sight unseen.

"No, Beverly. That's not him." Mackenzie sighed with her disappointment manifesting as irritation toward Beverly.

Beverley persisted with her efforts to marry Mackenzie off. "Well, do you think he's coming, Mackenzie? Maybe you should give him a call."

Mackenzie ignored her while Nate shot his wife a shut-the-hell-up look. Thank goodness, Beverly got the hint. Except for cheering on the boys, she was quiet the rest of the game.

The game ended in a three-point, season ending lost for the Eagles. They collected the kids with plans to accompany the rest of the team, their parents, and the coach to a nearby restaurant for pizza to celebrate the kids great season. Throughout the festivities, Mackenzie wondered in silence what happened to Andre. Her disappointment must have been written all over her face.

Just as they were finishing up and saying their goodbyes to the other parents, Andre called. His reason for not showing up on time was a premature labor. He apologized and said that he was less than two miles away from the stadium per his GPS. Romance revived, Mackenzie redirected him to the pizza restaurant.

"Hello. Sorry I'm late, everyone," Andre said, greeting Mackenzie with an embrace as he took a seat. He smelled just as good and was looking just as fine as Mackenzie remembered. He extended his hand to Nate and Beverly to formally introduce himself but was cut off by Beverly's excitement.

"No need to apologize, doctor. We know that obstetricians keep irregular schedules. I'm Mackenzie's sister-in-law, Beverly, this is her brother, my husband, Nathan, these are our children Jr., Jarvis, and

Ayana, and you of course know Mackenzie's angels. Beautiful children aren't they? How do you feel about kids doctor? Oh. Where are my manners? Would you like a slice of pizza?"

Amazingly, Beverly fired her inquiry at Andre in one breath, ending it by opening the box to offer him the now cold pizza.

Andre flashed Mackenzie a smile.

"No, thanks, I have already eaten. Yes, Mackenzie's children are beautiful, as are yours. And I love children. Anything else?" he laughed, shaking Nate's hand. "Nice to meet you, man."

"You too, Andre," Nate replied. "And don't pay any attention to my wife she's crazy."

"I am not." Beverly elbowed Nate. "I'm just being hospitable."

"You mean nosey," Nate corrected her.

Andre turned his attention to Traci with a hello, then to the boys and Ayana.

"I heard how hard you guys worked all this year, so I picked you up a little reward." He reached into the bag he brought with him and pulled out a new video game for each of them.

When Ayana asked, "What about me?" he produced an art set for her.

"I heard you like to draw," Andre said.

"That's so sweet. Isn't that sweet, Mackenzie?" Beverly said. "What do you say everyone?"

All the kids except Rashad said thank you and tore open the packaging.

Full of suspicion, Rashad glared at Andre. "Who are you? Are you my mom's boyfriend?" he bluntly asked, catching Andre off guard.

Mackenzie stepped in. "He's the friend mommy told you about, boo."

"Whatever," Rashad shrugged, uninterested in Andre or the gift, which he had pushed aside.

Mackenzie leaned in and whispered, "Thank you," to Andre.

"You're welcome," he whispered back.

Mackenzie's family enjoyed getting to know a little about Andre. Nate found someone who shared his love of fishing, larger than life SUV's, and all things football. Beverly not only discovered a potential match for Mackenzie, but someone else that she could impress with her cooking skills. Even Rashad's initial icy reception couldn't withstand Andre's charm. Nevertheless, when Traci had to break up a fight between Jarvis and Antwan, they knew that it was time to call it a night.

Nate and Beverly rounded up their children. They told Andre how nice it was to meet him and thanked him again for the gifts. Beverly also made sure to make him promise to come over for Sunday dinner. Andre said that he couldn't wait.

"Mom, let me have your keys," Traci said, sensing that her mother and Andre would like some time alone.

Mackenzie handed Traci her car keys. "I'll be just a minute longer."

"OK. Bye, Doc," Traci said to Andre.

"See you later, Traci," he smiled. He fist bumped the twins. "Later, little men."

Traci led the twins to the car.

"I'm glad you came. You had me worried for a minute."

"I'm sorry, I should have called earlier. Things get out of control quickly when dealing with premature childbirth," he said. "But, I'm glad I made it. Your family is great."

"Yeah, they are. Beverly didn't get on your nerves too much?"

Andre smiled. "No. You prepared me well." He hesitated, then reached for Mackenzie's hands. "Mackenzie, about the other night. I admit that I have some issues. My past still haunts me from time to time, but you are the first woman that I've gotten to know since, Rene died. I didn't expect to ever fall for anyone again. If you are willing to be patient, I know that we can really have something special."

He looked into her soulful eyes unsure of what she would say next.

After a moment, Mackenzie said, "I feel the same way, Andre. I think that we can have something special, too. I understand how you feel because moving on after Marlon died really seemed impossible. I didn't feel that I'd ever be ready. Who knows, maybe I'm still not, but I'm willing to try. Plus, something tells me not to give up on you so easily, Andre Lang."

Andre squeezed Mackenzie's hands. "You won't regret it," he said.

Rashad came rushing up to table. "Mom, are you and your boyfriend finished. We're ready to go home," he whined.

"Yes, boo," Mackenzie replied, stroking his head. Andre walked Mackenzie and her son to her car. He waved goodbye to them as they drove away feeling like his life was about to change for the better. Had he not been blinded by his new-found optimism, he might have noticed the man watched and plotted through his hate-filled eyes.

"What the hell are you talking about?" Captain Cedrick Baker asked. He shuffled through a pile of unorganized files on his desk, sucking the life out of a peppermint. "You quit? Get the hell out of my office and get back to your cases, Wilson. I got a shit load of work to do before I get out of here tonight. Plus, my wife's sister's in town, so I definitely don't need to hear your bitching right now. Lord knows, I got more than enough of it waiting for me at home."

"Carson, I'm serious. I honestly don't feel like I can do an effective job anymore. Its—"

Captain Baker slammed a thick file on his desk, cutting Keith off in mid-sentence. "Damn it, Wilson. Does this have something to do with the verdict in the Walter's trail?"

Keith's looked away. "It's more than that, sir," he said.

"You think that you are the only one that this shit has happened too? You've been on the force for what? Fourteen, fifteen years? You know better than anyone that guilty motherfuckers get off sometimes. As much as we'd like too, we can't win them all. The point is that we never stop trying our best. Now, you did your part. If anyone's to blame, it's the fucking DA's office."

"Captain, no disrespect. I just think that it's time for me to move on. I mean this job is really beginning to take a toll on me. The things I see. The sick people I deal with is becoming ingrained under my skin. I feel like I'm missing out on life. I don't want to end up as one of those burnt-out cops who resents the people that I swore to protect."

Keith watched Captain Baker shift through papers, seeming to have ignored everything Keith had just poured out. He glanced at the pictures of Baker's family and service awards that lined his office walls. Carson Baker was a fifty-something, warhorse who had been in the crime trenches for over three decades. Always a proud policeman, he had been known to subscribe to a hands-on approach to crime fighting. The scar across his left cheek given to him by a suspect his rookie year was evidence of that. Keith respected the man. He felt honored that Baker had taken him under his wing. Letting him down was something he didn't want.

When Captain Baker finally found what he was fumbling around for, he looked up at Keith. "Ok, Wilson. The fact is you are one of my best. You know that. I can't afford to lose you right now. Besides, who would take over your case load?"

"Parnell can handle them."

"Parnell?" he scoffed. "Parnell can barely wipe his ass without you. Be for real. Look, why don't we do this? Why don't you just take some time off? Take a nice two or three-week vacation to some beach where there's plenty of big tits and fat asses in your face to help you forget. How does that sound to you? Lord knows we all can use one."

Keith held his head back, sighing deeply as he pondered Captain Baker's suggestion.

Maybe a nice long vacation was all he needed.

Without warning Parnell burst into the office.

"What the hell, Leroy?" Captain Baker frowned.

"Sorry, Captain. Some big shit just happened at the Walter's estate. Turn on the news," Parnell said.

Baker reached for the remote to the wall mounted TV. A breaking news report showed several APD squad cars at the Walters' posh Buckhead family estate. The camera zoomed in on paramedics placing a body bag on a stretcher. It paned to a close-up of distraught members of the Walters family, then quickly shifted to the suspect handcuffed in the back of a squad car. Keith felt a sinking feeling when he realized that it was Barry Stewart.

A ginger headed female woman began her report.

"We are live at the Walters' family Buckhead estate where the father of Kendra Stewart, who real estate heir Thomas Walters was just acquitted of raping and murdering, has allegedly shot Thomas during a press conference the Walters family was holding to affirm

Thomas' acquittal. We want to warn you that the following is video is graphic."

Her introduction led to footage of the shocking incident. Thomas Walters stood at a podium on the front lawn of his home, his father and lawyers at his side. Bogus tears welled in his eyes, his greasy black hair glistened in the sunlight. He was giving a speech where he said that instead of running from the law he should have had faith in the justice system. Just as he had firmly stated that he could have never had done the terrible things that he was accused of doing, Barry Stewart materialized from the crowd.

Without so much as a peep, he marched toward Thomas. Two beefy security guards rushed him, taking him by either arm before he could get too close to their meal ticket.

"Let him go!" Thomas demanded, sending the media into a frenzy of murmurs and flashing cameras. The guards relinquished their hold. "He has already been through enough." Thomas extended his hand out to Barry. "Sir, I am so sorry that you had to lose your daughter that way. I can't imagine what you are going through, but I pledge here and now that you have the full assistance of the Walters family in finding her true killers."

"I don't need no help," Barry Stewart said. He was calm and clear. "I know who killed my baby girl." Faster than the security guards could react, Barry whipped a 9mm pistol from inside his jacket. He quickly pumped two bullets into Thomas' chest, sending the lawn full of people scrambling for cover. Too late to stop the lethal damage, the security guards pounced on Barry and the elder Walters made a valiant effort to shield his blood splattered son from further harm.

Keith turned to Captain Baker, who was transfixed by the startling events on the TV screen. "You'll have my official resignation on your desk first thing in the morning, sir," he said.

CHAPTER 16

Happiness...Joy...Love...Hope. The words wailed in his mind. Sweat dripped from his naked, sinewy body onto the tattered musty couch. Those were words meant for people who deserved it. Not Lang. He stabbed his long hunting knife into a photo that he had taken of Andre and Mackenzie while they were leaving the Fox Theater.

Scattered throughout the filthy carpet and pinned along the dingy walls of the tiny, dank apartment were other pictures of Andre. Each one giving him more reasons to hate the man. More reasons to make him suffer.

"He thinks he deserves to be happy after the shit he did to me?" he grumbled. "Who does that motherfucker think he is?" He exploded with a final fatal stab to Andre's photo. A powerful kick sent the flimsy coffee table flying across the room.

Happiness...Joy...Love...Hope. He could hear laughter coming from the pictures on the walls, sending him into a dizzying rage. He sprang from the couch and ripped down the photos that taunted him with tales of Andre's newfound happiness. The laughter echoed and multiplied until he felt surrounded. *Happiness...Joy...Love...Hope.* He covered his ears to shut it out. It didn't work. *Happiness...Joy...Love... Hope.*

"Fuck you. It won't last," he yelled at the photos. "It won't last."

Silence.

He had to make Lang suffer until he begged to die. A picture on the floor, partially covered by a moldy pizza box, caught his eye. It was Andre standing outside of his house talking with his neighbor.

That nosey old bitch. He frowned and crumpled the photo in his hand. The laughter was about to end.

––––––––––––

"Dr. Lang here is that patient's file you wanted," Paula said, placing a folder on Andre's desk. Busy reviewing another patient's dismal laboratory results, Andre acknowledged Paula with an inaudible mumble.

Paula watched him as he worked. A new picture on his desk showed him posing with Mackenzie caught her eye. They looked happy together. Paula had noticed a change in Dr. Lang in the few weeks since they had been seeing each other. Before he seemed as if he had been forcing himself to smile. Since Mackenzie came into his life his smiles were genuine.

They obviously care for one another and Mackenzie is good for him, Paula thought. *Too bad they were living in sin.*

"Did you need something else, Paula?" Andre asked, noticing that she was still in his office.

"Yes, doctor. I wanted to invite you to my church tonight. We are having a guest speaker. I'm not sure what the sermon is supposed to be about, but she is usually very inspiring. And I think you could use a little Jesus." She smiled.

Andre was surprised that it had taken Paula this long to start inviting him to church events. "Paula, I would love too."

Paula's face lit up. "Really?"

"Yes, I would. Just not this time. I already have plans with friends."

"You can bring them all along. Don't tell me you're all too busy for the Lord," Paula responded.

"Of course not, Paula. But really, some other time," Andre said, flipping through the file she had brought in.

Paula accepted his answer and left his office in a small huff. Andre could tell that she wanted to preach to him some more.

Andre's cell phone rang. It was his therapist. No doubt she was calling to find out why he had canceled his last three sessions and why he had not bothered to reschedule.

"Hello, Roslyn," he answered.

"Andre, darling. This is Dr. Lewis, your therapist. You do remember me, don't you?" She half-chuckled.

"Vaguely." He joked. "How are you, Roslyn?"

"I'm fine, darling. It's you that I'm concerned about. Why is it that you have not scheduled an appointment with me as of late?"

Andre squirmed in his chair. He knew that Dr. Lewis would come down on him when she heard his rationale. "I've been meaning to call you. I have decided that it's time that I discontinued our sessions."

"Oh? And why is that, Andre. Have I done or said something that was displeasing to you?"

"Not at all. It's just that I feel that I need to work through this without you to fall back on. Don't worry you have given me all the coping tools that I need. And Mackenzie—"

"OK. Listen, Andre," she said, cutting him off. "I am happy that you and Mackenzie are still seeing each other. Really, I am. But you still have some very serious issues that require the aid of a qualified therapist. If not me, then someone else. You went through a very terrible ordeal and without proper psychological help, it will surely continue to affect every aspect of your life."

Firmly, Andre replied, "Thank you doctor, but I have made my decision."

"And so, you have." She sighed. "For the record, I think that you are making a mistake. I will be here when you need me."

After seven, Blu Cantina was a very different place. Instead of the loud happy hour crowd, the customers were more subdued. Mackenzie and Joel were seated on the second level waiting for Andre and his friend Ethan Carlson. Ethan lived in Houston but was in the process of being relocated to Atlanta for a job with a new law firm.

Andre and Ethan's history went back to their undergrad roommate days at Tennessee State. Ethan had stunned Andre by revealing his sexuality after his disgruntled ex-boyfriend threaten to out him. At the time, Andre's image of gay men was defined only by flamboyant stereotypes, not by someone masculine and confident like Ethan. At first Ethan's sexuality made Andre uncomfortable, but they quickly developed a strong friendship. Ethan became one of the people that Andre credited with opening his eyes to no matter anyone's sexual orientation: Love is love.

"I'm not so sure about this, Z," Joel said, looking around the restaurant for Andre and his mystery friend. "I don't like being set up on blind dates…especially by a straight man. Andre don't know if Ethan is cute or not." He snatched up a tortilla chip and dipped it in salsa. "How do I look by the way?"

Mackenzie glanced over at him. "You look just as nice as when I saw you in this outfit the first couple times," Mackenzie chuckled, brushing lint from his distressed denim shirt. "And I told you that I saw pictures of Ethan. He's very attractive."

"Please. Aren't those pictures over fifteen years old? You forgot to add in the extra four or five inches to his waistline and subtract about two inches from his hair line."

Mackenzie chuckled, crutching on a chip. "Well, I have seen some of your dates lately, so I'm sure that you wouldn't mind hanging out with a fat balding man for a couple of hours."

"Whatever."

"Here they come."

Joel glanced over and saw Andre walking up the winding staircase. He was being followed by a handsome dude wearing a grey cable knit sweater, mid blue ripped jeans, and camel Timberland boots.

Joel nudged Mackenzie. "OK. OK. Score one for, Andre," he whispered.

"Told you."

"What's up good people?" Andre slid next to Mackenzie and pulled her in for a kiss. Ethan sat across from Joel.

"Get a room," Joel said.

Andre laughed. "Joel, this is my good friend, Ethan. Ethan this is Joel."

"Nice to meet you," they both said in their deepest voices, shaking hands.

Mackenzie smiled. It was obvious that Ethan and Joel were impressed with one another. Ethan was tall with copper bronze skin and muscles that bulged from underneath his sweater. A cool, fauxhawk blended into the neat beard framing his sculpted features. Smiling with his slanted eyes and thick groomed eyebrows made it hard to look away from him.

"And this is my lady, Mackenzie," Andre said.

Ethan tore his gaze away from Joel long enough to greet Mackenzie.

"So, I finally get to place a face with the lady that my boy has been going on and on about," Ethan said, shaking Mackenzie's hand. "And I can see why. You're gorgeous."

"Thank you," Mackenzie said, squeezing Ethan's bicep. "Andre said you were into bodybuilding."

Ethan replied, "Not nearly as much as anymore but I still try to do a little something."

Andre wrapped his arms around Mackenzie's shoulders. "Hey, hey. Don't be trying to push up on my girl, man."

"Don't worry," Ethan said, returning his attention back to Joel. "I see someone that I can focus on."

Andre laughed. "Let's get this party started." He waved over the waiter to order a pitcher of margaritas and a hookah.

The night continued with lots of feel-good laughter, amazing food, and plenty of drinks as they got to know each other. Since Ethan's father was a Swedish national and his mother South African, his family had moved to New York City from South Africa when he was a toddler to escape apartheid. He settled in Houston after law school at Duke to become a defense attorney. Andre and Ethan reminisced on their crazy undergrad days at Tennessee State. Nude modeling for art students to earn a few dollars, or Andre getting caught hiding a girl under his bed by the R.A. was especially funny.

They had started on their third pitcher when Mackenzie spotted Keith seated at the bar on the lower level. He was alone, throwing back a nice sized drink as if was planning on solving his troubles at the bottom of a glass. Mackenzie couldn't stand to see him that way.

"Excuse me," Mackenzie said to everyone. "Be right back."

"Another one, please," Keith said to the bartender, as he drained the last drops of Tequila from his glass. "Better yet, just leave the bottle."

"Tough day at the office, huh?" The bartender chuckled.

"You don't know the half," Keith said.

"You wanna talk about it?" The bartender asked, refilling Keith's glass.

"Nah, man. Just keep the drinks coming." Talking about anything having to do with the APD was the last thing that Keith wanted to do. Drowning in the soothing burn of alcohol until he couldn't remember anything was the better option. No matter how temporary his amnesia would be.

Today he had received an emotional call from Mrs. Greta Bradford. She demanded to know what progress the police had made in finding her daughter's murderer. Dana Bradford's gutted body lying in the middle of Piedmont Park flashed in his mind. To date, there were no leads in her case. Forensics had come up empty. No witnesses had come forward and none of Dana's friends could offer any insight into who would have wanted to harm her.

Keith was sorry to have to report that there were no new developments in her daughter's case. She broke down, picturing her child's last moments, pleading for her life. Butchered by a heartless killer. Keith promised Mrs. Bradford that he would commit all the time that he could to making sure Dana would not end up a cold case, filed away, and forgotten.

Why the fuck did I become a cop? he thought, looking at his phone. *And where the fuck is Parnell?* Parnell was a good forty-five minutes late. The only reason that he was throwing back drinks at Blu Cantina was because Parnell had said that he was feeling kind of down and wanted to get out for a drink. Keith didn't believe him for a second. He knew that Parnell's true motives were to try to bring Keith out of his funk. Good ole loyal, Parnell.

Mackenzie tapped Keith on the shoulder. He jerked around expecting to see Parnell with some lame excuse as to why he was late.

"Hey, man, where the fuc—?" He caught himself in mid-sentence. Where Parnell should have been, his love interest stood in his place, looking as flawless as always.

"Don't tell me that you're going to curse me out again," she smiled, referring to the day at the courthouse when Keith had mistakenly yelled profanities at her. "I already let you get away with it once before, don't try your luck, again, detective."

"Mackenzie," Keith said, turning back to his drink. "I've been meaning to call you. So much was happening. I didn't recognize your voice. I'm really sorry about that."

Mackenzie took a seat on the barstool next to him. "No big deal. You were under a lot of stress. Actually, I've been worried about you. I know how important it was for you to get justice for the Stewart family. But then to have Barry Stewart arrested for killing Thomas Walters on top of it." She rubbed his shoulder to console him. "With all that has happened, are you OK?"

Damn her touch felt good. "Yeah, win some, lose some. Let down a lot of people in the process. This is the life I choose."

"Don't be so hard on yourself. You've done a lot of good, Keith."

Keith took a swig of drink. "I guess. I really wanted to put that smug motherfucker away," he said. "Excuse my language. It was just so unbelievable when the jury found him not guilty. Now that POS is dead. Mrs. Stewart has lost both her daughter *and* maybe her husband, too." He shook his head. "Some top cop I turned out to be, right?"

"Why are being so hard on yourself?" Mackenzie asked. "These things happen."

"Tameka Akins," Keith whispered, staring into his drink.

"Who?"

He turned to face her. "Tameka Akins, a family friend from back home in Alabama. We grew up like brother and sister."

"OK. What about her?"

"She needed me to pick her up from her after school job one night. I told her that I was coming, but I was too busy fucking off with some chick. She walked by herself. That was the last time anyone ever saw her alive." He swirled his glass as he looked down. "They found her body about a week later rotting in a ditch. She had been raped. Strangled. I should have been there for her."

"Keith," Mackenzie consoled him.

"She's the reason I became a cop," he continued. "Guess I never got over the guilt. But you know what? I don't want to talk about that. You look real nice tonight, Mackenzie. What's the occasion?"

"Nothing special. Just hanging out."

"OK. You here with Joel?" Keith asked, preparing to take a swallow of his drink.

"Yeah. Joel and a couple of other friends," Mackenzie said just as Andre appeared behind her as if on cue.

"There you are," Andre said, walking up behind Mackenzie. "We were beginning to think that you had gotten lost."

Mackenzie said, "I spotted an old friend. Dr. Andre Lang this is Detective Keith Wilson."

"Hey, nice to meet you, man," Andre said, shaking Keith's hand. "Any friend of my lady is a friend of mine."

Lady. The word hit Keith like a kick to the balls. Still, he smiled and nodded as though he were unaffected. "You too, man. So, what type of doctor are you, Andrew?"

"It's Andre. And I'm an obstetrician/gynecologist."

If Andre went on to babble about whatever the fuck he did for a living, Keith heard none of it. He could only see the way Andre caressed Mackenzie's shoulders, and the way Mackenzie clasped Andre's hand. *Dr. Andre Lang,* Keith thought while sizing him up. A corny, pretty boy. Keith wanted to punch him right in his capped teeth. *What's Mackenzie doing with a lame ass dude like that?*

"We should get back to Joel and Ethan," Mackenzie said to Andre. "Keith, it was good seeing you again."

"You too, Mackenzie." Keith fake smiled, picturing himself grabbing her, and drop kicking Andre.

"See you around, man," Andre waved said seemed as he and Mackenzie left.

Once again Keith watched the woman that he loved walk away, only this time she was in the arms of another man. A few more minutes had passed with still no sign of Parnell.

"Excuse me is someone sitting here?" Keith heard a woman ask, just as he was sending Parnell another text.

She sat on stool next to him before he could answer. Keith checked her out. She was a pretty, curvy chick in her late twenties or early thirties with heavy makeup over carmel skin. A luxurious weave cascaded down her back and a low-cut black dress gripped her large breast.

"No. Help yourself," Keith said.

"Don't tell me you're drinking alone tonight, sexy," she asked.

"Looks like it."

"We can't have that," she said, winking at Keith and motioning for the bartender. "I'll have whatever he's having. And put it on his tab. He looks like he could use a drinking buddy."

"I'll take another one too," Keith said.

"So, are we drinking out of regret or to forget?" she asked.

Keith leaned into to her as the bartender sat their drinks in front of them. She smelled like peaches. "Pick one," he said. *Fuck it.*

CHAPTER 17

Butterflies churned in her stomach as Mackenzie checked herself out in Andre's bathroom mirror. She turned her shapely figure to the left then to the right, sucking in a little here, pushing up a little there, satisfied with how she looked in her pink lace bra and pantie set.

After leaving Blu Cantina, she and Andre talked about taking their relationship to the next level. The fun outing and bottomless pitchers of margaritas helped Mackenzie drop the reservations she had from their first failed attempt at lovemaking.

"Do I have to come in there, baby?" Mackenzie heard Andre yell from his bedroom.

"Just a second. You know, you should have a little more patience. Good things come to those who wait."

"Yeah, well, sleep comes to those who wait too long," Andre replied.

"Whatever." She checked her hair, then reached in her bag to spray a little perfume between her breast before stepping into the bedroom.

Andre had his room glowing from what seemed like dozens of red candles. Miguel's *Adorn* playing added another touch of romance. A trail of rose petals led to the bed where Andre lay wearing only a pair of black briefs.

"Still sleepy?" Mackenzie asked, leaning in the doorway,

Andre sat up, appreciating Mackenzie's hourglass figure, ample breast, and plump ass peaking from her panties. She twirled her hair over her left eye like a flirty wink. "Nope. Wide awake," he said. "Come here, baby."

She picked up one of the petals from the floor. "Rose petals?"
"Corny?"

"Just a little," she chuckled, sliding into bed next to him. "But I'll overlook it, 'cause you're kinda sexy."

Andre handed her a flute of champagne. "You think I'm sexy, huh?" he asked, kissing her neck.

"You'll do," Mackenzie teased him, trying to pretend that Andre's lips didn't send electric sensations down her spine.

"I'll do?" Andre laughed. "I saw you checking out Ethan, but woman you better take a good look at this body." He stood up to flex his chiseled hairless chest and well-toned biceps.

Mackenzie took another sip then sat the glass on the nightstand. "Let me show you how sexy you are," she said, patting the bed.

Andre lay on top of her, stroking her honey brown cheek, finding solace in her eyes.

"You're a beautiful soul, Mackenzie," he said.

"Thanks, but you didn't say anything about my lingerie. I wore it just for you."

"Nice baby, but I'd take you naked," he chuckled, pulling her closer. Mackenzie whimpered as Andre kissed his way from her neck to her shoulders. He pulled down her bra to access her nipples as he wiggled out of his briefs.

"Andre," she whimpered. Her body went limp from the attention he paid to her breast. In vain, she stroked his hard penis to return the pleasure to him. Andre would have none of it. Tonight, was all about pleasing Mackenzie. He gently pushed her back against the bed, sliding off her panties to continue his oral discovery of her body. The melody of her moaning made his dick throb with each kiss he planted across her flat stomach and sensitive inner thighs. He teased her a little before his mouth found her throbbing clit. She arched her back as Andre tasted her. Just when she felt that she was about to explode, he pulled her up onto his thighs. She lost herself in his soft lips, wrapping herself around his body, guiding his erection into her wetness. Rocking chest to breast, they enjoyed sensations that had been too long neglected.

Andre lay back enjoying the sight of Mackenzie riding his dick. She threw her head back slowly, savoring the moment. In rhythm to the conversation of their bodies, he thrust his hardness deep into her juices.

"Andre." she moaned, moving faster.

Andre sat up to embrace her, mouthing her breast, cupping her soft ass. "Come for me, baby," he whispered.

"You too."

He glided his fingers along her lips as she leaned back, gripping him with her thighs. Feeling him hit all the right spots, she let herself free, clawing his back, every atom of her body caught in the explosion. He erupted inside of her, each contraction matching her moans.

"Shit. Mackenzie." They locked lips, orgasming in harmony, quivering in the aftermath.

Mackenzie collapsed on the bed. After a moment of gasping for air, she sat up.

"Don't tell me you're tapped out already," she asked.

He pulled her to him and flipped her over on her stomach. "Just warming up," he whispered in her ear.

———————

Keith slowly awoke to the smell of bacon frying and what sounded like pots banging in a kitchen. A roaring hangover scrambled his memories of the previous night.

"Shit," he groaned as his vision flickered into focus, revealing a bedroom that was not his. Adding to the mystery, a fuzzy pink blanket swaddled him like warm cotton candy. Gripping his forehead, he rolled over, straight into the barrel of a gun looming at his forehead.

"Fuck," he yelled, diving over the side of the bed, raising his hands in surrender. "Police officer. Don't shoot."

After what seemed like an eternity, he heard a child laughing, followed by a water stream splattering his face.

"Got you." The child giggled loudly.

"Tarrick? What are you doing?" A woman in a short fuchsia robe rushed into the room. "Give me this," she said, snatching the water gun away from him. "Go downstairs and eat your breakfast, boy."

"Sorry mommy. I was just playing with your friend." The chubby little boy pouted.

Shit, Keith exhaled. As he watched the woman shoo her son away, he remembered where he was, and what went down the night before: Too much self-doubt mixed with lots of tequila had led to him coming home with the girl that he had met at Blu Cantina. Plenty of raunchy sex had followed. The kind one had when they were trying to forget something or someone. Two empty gold condom wrappers on the nightstand told him that at least they had been safe.

"Hey, sorry about that," the woman said. "You know how kids are these days."

"No problem." Keith stood up, realizing that he was naked. "Where are my clothes?"

She sat on the bed, admiring Keith's broad shoulders and tall chiseled body. He snatched up a pillow to cover his dick.

"Mmmm. Don't be shy, now. I already know what you're working with." She smirked.

"I just got to get going."

"What's the rush, sexy?" she asked, biting her bottom lip. "I can go another round...or two." She moved to close the bedroom door. "Cops need lovin too, don't they?"

Yeah, they do. Just not from you, Keith thought, thinking of seeing Mackenzie at the restaurant last night in the arms of that corny dude. He spotted his clothes and shoes on a chair in the corner. "Last night was fun, um...Jasmine, but I've got to get going. Maybe some other time," he said, getting dressed.

"It's Jamesha." She opened her robe. "Are you sure about that? I don't know how we could out do last night, but you got this bomb ass pussy standing in front of you to try again."

Keith took in her voluptuous body. Sex with Jasmine, Jamesha, or whatever the hell her name was what he needed last night, but he had way more important things to worry about today. Besides, the gun was a toy this time, but things could have turned out differently.

"As tempting as that sounds, yeah, I'm sure. Some other time."

"Diarrhea from food poisoning?" Keith laughed at Parnell over the phone. "You feeling better?"

"Not really, man. I think I got it from this random Chinese restaurant this chick took me to for lunch. You know that's the worst kind to get." He groaned. "I still got the bubble guts."

Keith laughed. "Good reason to flake on me."

"My bad." Parnell said. "What'd you end up doing?"

"I got drunk. Went home with some girl I met at the restaurant."

"Damn, bro. That's not like you. Was she fine at least?" Parnell laughed.

"I guess," Keith said, recalling Jamesha.

"I thought you were feeling that reporter, Mackenzie, anyway."

"Yeah, well shit doesn't always go the way you want," Keith replied. "I saw her with this dude at the restaurant. They're together. Guess I missed my chance."

"Man, don't sweat it. There're plenty girls I could hook you up with. Atlanta is full of easy pussy."

"I'm not worried about that right now," Keith said as he got out of his car. "I'm getting ready to question someone about a new development in the Dana Bradford case. Hit me later, shitty."

"Fuck you," Parnell chuckled, hanging up.

Keith had promised Dana Bradford's mother to focus on solving her murder. He had other cases that needed to be reassigned before leaving the police force, but there was something about this particular case that drew him in. There weren't very many leads he could go on, so he had questioned Dana's best friend, Sonya Norman, and coworker Mary Wu again. They weren't useful that day, but later Mary helped him get a break in the case.

A call late one evening changed the direction of the case.

"Detective Wilson, this is Mary Wu."

"Yes, Mary. How can I help you?" he asked cheerlessly.

"I have been doing some thinking, and I feel that there is something you need to know about Dana."

Keith's ears perked up as he grabbed a pen. "OK. I'm listening," he replied, surprised that the lead would come from the seemingly heartless Mary Wu.

"It may be nothing, and I could lose my job for telling you this." Mary took a long pause. "Dana was having an affair with our company's president, Quincy Miller."

"Oh, really?"

"Yes," Mary told him. "She said that they had been seeing each other for about six months"

"How do you know this?"

"Dana got really drunk at an office party we attended the week before she was murdered. She was way too messed up to take an Uber alone, so I took her home," Mary said. "She told me everything on the ride to her place, then swore me to secrecy the next day at the office."

"Did Dana ever say that she expected Quincy to leave his wife for her?" Keith had asked. He knew that threatening to expose infidelity was a timeless motive for murder.

"No, nothing like that. She said that she was just using him to get ahead. Neither of them had any expectations," Mary replied. "I honestly don't even know if she was telling the truth about any of it."

"I see," he said, circling Quincy's name. "Well, thank you for coming forward with this information, Mary, every little bit helps."

"Wait, detective, there is something else you should know. Dana also told me that Quincy had gotten her pregnant and that she had an abortion."

Keith stepped into the crowed elevator. *This may pan out to be something,* he hoped.

———————

"I want to know every filthy detail," Joel insisted over the phone as Mackenzie strolled through busy Ponce City Market toward the elevator banks.

"I can't tell you every detail," she said, recalling the sizzling evening of loving making she had shared with Andre. "Maybe just the G-rated version."

"Hey, I'll take whatever I can get." Joel laughed. "Just as long as I know you're finally gettin' some."

"Mmmm. Yes-I-am," Mackenzie moaned, turning a corner. She immediately, spotted Keith looking over the building directory posted across from the elevators. "Let me call you back." Mackenzie hung up before Joel could protest.

"Hey, Keith. This is a surprise bumping into you again," she said. "Are you following me?"

Keith turn around. *Mackenzie.* What a coincidence running into her today after seeing her all lovey-dovey with Dr. 'What's-his-face' the other night. The guilt that he felt from going home with that girl didn't help either.

He laughed. "Good morning, Mackenzie. What are you doing over here this early?"

"Chasing a story. And I couldn't resist catching sale or two of course," she said, holding up two boutique bags. "What about you?"

"Following up on a lead in the Dana Bradford case. Turns out that there are some new developments."

"Really?" She smiled, elbowing him. "Are you sharing, detective? Strictly off the record, of course."

"Well, it turns out that Dana was having an affair with her boss," Keith said.

"Oh?"

"Not only that, but she had gotten pregnant by him. She had an abortion a few days before she was killed. I'm going to question the guy. See if it leads anywhere."

"Pregnant? But wouldn't that have come up in Dana's toxicology report?"

"You would think," Keith frowned. "Looks like the incompetent medical examiner's office messed up big time. I have already had a nice frank discussion with them. This case might have been solved a long time ago."

"Right," Mackenzie agreed. She glanced at Keith. The alluring confidence he normally had was permanently replaced with the same doubt she saw in him at the Blu Cantina. "Are you feeling better?"

"Yeah. I'm fine," he said, and then hesitated. "I've decided to leave the force."

"What? Why, Keith? I thought police work was your calling."

"I thought so, too. Once. Now, I'm not so sure. Maybe I have another calling," he said, looking into her eyes. "Everything going well with you?"

He hoped that she would say something that would include the phrase: *I'm done with lame ass Andre.* Instead the elevator chimed, and a bunch of people shuffled out. Mackenzie was glad for the interruption because she didn't have the heart to tell Keith that her life was going great in comparison to his. Work was as rewarding as ever. Her children couldn't be happier, and she and Andre were getting closer every day. Life was good.

"You know. Same ole, same ole," she shrugged, entering the elevator. "Take care of yourself, Keith. Give me a call if you ever need someone to talk to."

"I might just do that." He half-smiled as the doors shut. *I might just do that.*

CHAPTER 18

Quincy Miller was a jerk. Keith knew from the first two minutes of speaking to him. He was a stout man in his early fifties, oozing a textbook case of a Napoleon complex, and seemed to believe that people used the bathroom stall next to him just to smell his shit. He basked in his position as president of UNINET—the bullied, fat kid who finally got his revenge.

Money and power, Keith thought. *Probably the only reason he could get a girl like Dana.*

"Yes, detective Wilson," Quincy said after beating around the bush. "Dana and I were having an affair."

Quincy waddled over to the credenza in the corner of his office and poured himself a cup of coffee. He didn't bother to offer Keith any. "What's the big deal?"

Keith was getting irritated. "The big deal is that she aborted your baby a few days before she was killed. Care to elaborate?"

Quincy returned to his desk and sipped a steaming cup.

"There's nothing more to say. We screwed a few times. Got careless once. She got pregnant. Abortion was the only option. Dana was focused on her career and as you probably already know, I'm married with two children," he said, pointing to a photo of his wife and kids. All three looked like they could shut down an all-you-can-eat buffet.

"So, the decision to abort was mutual?"

"Of course. Dana and I both knew that a child was absolutely out of the question." He took a sip of coffee. "Do you mind telling me if you plan to go public with this, Detective Wilson? I mean there's no need. Knowledge of our little occasional roll in the hay can't do anything to help solve this case."

"Maybe. Maybe not," Keith said. "I just find it more than coincidental that this was done to a girl that had just had an abortion a few days before she was murdered." Keith tossed a photo of Dana's gutted corpse onto Quincy's desk. "The killer raped, suffocated her, then ripped out her uterus."

"Jesus," Quincy whispered clearly taken aback by the image. He studied them for a few seconds before he spoke. "What kind of a monster would do this Dana?"

"That's what I need your help to find out," Keith replied. "So, you need to stop thinking of yourself and stop worrying if people will find out that you were fucking her so that we can take whoever did this off the streets."

Quincy rubbed his hands through his thinning grey hair. "I don't know anything. I barley even know that much about Dana. Our affair was just that casual."

Keith sprang from the chair and slapped another photo down on the desk. This one showed Quincy a close-up of Dana's lifeless eyes glaring back at him.

"You need to think hard Quincy," Andre said, his voice threatening. "Did Dana ever mention that she was seeing someone else? What about a jealous boyfriend?"

"No, nothing, detective." He sobbed. "I have told you everything that I know."

Keith glared at the pitiful man crying. For all his bravado, Quincy probably was about to piss himself.

"Who is the doctor that she went to get her abortion?" Keith asked a little more calmly. "We have already questioned her usual gynecologist. She said that she did not perform the procedure."

"I don't know that either. Dana said that she would take care of it. I gave her cash and that was the last I heard of it until now."

Keith sighed, watching Quincy wipe away tears. He could see that he wasn't getting anything useful out of him today. He collected the photos. "Here is my card. Call me if anything comes to mind. And I do plan on speaking to your human resources department to see if Dana or anyone else had any sexual harassment claims against you. So, this isn't over," he said just to put more fear in Quincy. "I haven't ruled you out as a suspect."

Just as he turned to leave, Quincy stopped him.

"Wait, Detective," he said, rummaging through his desk drawers. He pulled out a copy of *Elle* magazine. "I forgot that Dana gave me this as a joke. She wanted me to read the article on how a wife knows her husband's cheating or something."

"So. What's this got to do with anything?" Keith shrugged, reaching for the magazine.

"Look at the name of who it's addressed."

Keith glanced at the mailing label. He instantly recognized the name that had been stuck in his head for the past few days: Dr. Andre Q. Lang, OB/GYN.

_____

"Who's at my door this time of night?" Mrs. Russell wondered, squinting through her peep hole.

"Sorry to bother you, ma'am," the young man smiled. "My finance and I just moved in across the street. I'm so stupid I locked myself out and my cell phone is dead. May I use your phone really quick?"

Emma Russell grew up during the depression. To go without was the rule rather than the exception, especially for black families in the Jim Crow South. Her single mother struggled to earn a few pennies washing white people's laundry when she could. Often, it was only through the kindness of neighbors that meant the difference between Emma and her siblings starving. Their selflessness imprinted young Emma with the belief to always give of yourself, even if it meant sacrifice on your part. With that guidance, she had no problem offering her assistance to the stranger.

"Sure," she said. "You must be the couple that just rented the Stokes place. Just a moment, young man."

After a minute or so she came back to hand him her phone through the cracked door. He pushed hard against it, knocking her to the ground. He slammed the door shut and was slicing her throat before she could process what was happening or scream for help.

"Nosey bitch," he sneered, spitting on the poor old women's bloody corpse. He sat down, lighting a cigarette as he surveyed the neat house, which smelled of vanilla and Bengay. *This will do just fine.*

Mrs. Emma Rosemary Russell, widow, community activist, and surrogate grandmother of Dr. Andre Q. Lang was 78 years old when she died as she lived: helping someone in need.

_____

"I may be over a little late tonight, baby," Andre said to Mackenzie over the speakerphone. He was clicking through files on his computer. "Ethan needs me to pick him up from the airport."

"Why can't Joel do it?" Mackenzie wondered, throwing her laundry in the dryer. Joel and Ethan had been seeing each other a lot from what Joel had told her.

"Ethan has been out of town. He's taking the redeye from Phoenix tonight to surprise Joel, so don't go running your mouth." Andre smiled.

"That's right. Joel did mention that Ethan was away on business. Alright, boo. Make sure you hurry. I've got something special planned for you," Mackenzie said in a silly intimate voice.

"Are you trying to seduce me, ma'am?"

"Don't get too cocky, sir. I might just need you to change the oil in my car."

Andre chuckled. "See you tonight, baby."

"OK." She hung up and texted Nate to make sure that the twins were behaving themselves. They were staying at Nate's for the weekend. Traci was at school with her pre-SAT study group. Mackenzie texted her to remind her to check in when it was over, then take an Uber to Nate's house. She got back to doing laundry. She found a pair of Andre's briefs mixed with her stuff in the hamper. In the family room, she put away the video game controllers that Andre and the twins had used the day before. Mackenzie smiled at the reminders that Andre had been spending more time at her house. Having him around felt good. Natural.

Her cell phone rang as she was cleaning the kitchen. It was Keith. She quickly answered.

"Hi, Keith."

"Hey, Mackenzie. How have you been?"

"I've been good," she said. "What about you?"

Good because of Dr. Wonderful no doubt. "I've been OK," he couldn't help but reply in a tone that Mackenzie picked up on.

"Are you sure? You don't sound like it."

"Yeah. I'm just tired, I guess. Been running around trying to get things in order before I leave the force," he said.

"So, you are really going to leave?" she asked, sitting down.

"Yeah," he sighed. "It's time to move on. Time to find another way to fight the good fight."

"Any idea what you are going to do next?"

"As far as a career is concerned, I haven't thought that far ahead. I enjoy working with at risk kids, though. In the meantime, I have some money saved up from a few investments, so I plan on doing some traveling. I'm thinking Asia and Africa."

"Sounds good. I'm sure the trip will help you figure things out."

"That's what I'm hoping. But listen, Mackenzie I was just calling to check up on you and say hello," he lied. "So, I won't take up too much of your time."

"I really appreciate that, Keith. Don't be a stranger."

"I won't. Take care, Mackenzie." Keith hung up and let out a hard sigh. He could hear the happiness in her voice, so he had held back his true reason for calling to warn her about Andre's possible connection to a murder. He wanted no part in taking happiness away from her, especially since he had not established a clear connection to Andre and Dana Bradford. More than ever Keith needed to solve this case. For all he knew Mackenzie's life may depend on it.

The bathroom glowing from candlelight, Mackenzie and Andre were relaxing in the spa tub sipping red wine, and taking each other in. Cassandra Wilson's sultry delivery of *You Move Me* dripped like warm honey over the speakers. Mackenzie was seated between Andre's legs, her head rested against his chest. He massaged her shoulders as warm, frothy lavender scented water indulged their bodies. If things could get any better neither of them could see how. Still, Mackenzie could not help but to think about the earlier phone call she had received from Keith. She had not wanted to push him to talk, but she could tell that he wanted to reach out to her. Vent about what he was going through, full of doubt as he fought to right wrongs in the world.

"Are you OK, baby?" Andre asked, pulling Keith from her thoughts.

Mackenzie turned to face him. "I'm fine. Perfect," she said. "Why do you ask?"

"You tensed up all of a sudden."

"Oh. I was just thinking about a friend," she replied, laying back against his chest.

"Anyone I know?"

"Keith Wilson. You remember meeting him at Blu Cantina, don't you?"

"The detective, right?" Andre continued to rub her shoulders. "I didn't want to ask before, but what's the story between you two?"

"He's just an old friend. We went out once."

"Ok. What's got you zoned out thinking about him? I don't have a reason to be jealous, do I?" Andre smiled.

"No," Mackenzie said. "Keith just seems to be going through some things right now. He even quit the APD."

"Why'd he do that?"

"He didn't say outright, but I'm guessing it's because he feels that he no longer making a difference," she sighed. "And when Thomas

Walters got off for murdering, Kendra Stewart, then Kendra's father killed Thomas, I think it sent him over the edge."

Guilt, Andre thought, something that he knew all about.

Mackenzie continued. "Now he is pouring all his energy into solving the Dana Bradford murder before he leaves the force. Do you remember hearing about her? It was all over the news."

"Vaguely," Andre replied. He reached for his wine glass next to the tub. "I try not to watch the news much. It's been getting too depressing. Wasn't she found murdered in Piedmont Park a few months back?"

"Right?"

"I'm not trying to be callous, baby," Andre said, taking a sip. "But that type of thing must happen all the time in Atlanta. Why is Keith so concerned with this particular case?"

"Well, I'm not supposed to talk about it, but Dana wasn't just raped and killed. Mackenzie paused as thoughts of the appalling murder slithered on her skin. "She was raped, suffocated then the killer cut her open and ripped out her uterus."

Andre went ghost white. Mackenzie's voice faded into a distant murmur as the wine glass slipped from his trembling hand, shattering against the bathroom floor.

———

Sleep did not come to Andre. Mackenzie's revelation about what really had happened to Dana Bradford peeled away the scab over his heart. His mind swirled with thoughts of Rene and Zhuri. Closing his eyes conjured unnerving memories of his frantic search after coming home from the office to find them gone, calling friends and family members, knocking on neighbor's doors, contacting the nonchalant police. Finally, dragging himself from the police station that cold

November day to find the love of his life and their only child dead. Raped, suffocated, and gutted. Just like Dana Bradford.

Careful not to disturb Mackenzie, Andre crept out of bed to the bathroom. He slumped on the floor, his hands on his forehead. *What was happening?* Surely the way that Dana was killed could not have been a simple coincidence. He gasped. *What if whoever killed them followed me to Atlanta and had also killed Dana.* He cracked the bathroom door to glimpse Mackenzie sleeping peacefully. *What if I am putting her and her kids in danger just by being in their lives?*

"Why won't this nightmare end?" Andre wept. "What did I do wrong?"

No answers came to him. Only excruciating silence along with it the one thing he knew for certain: It was time he told Mackenzie the truth.

CHAPTER 19

Keith wasted no time. He had found out about the abduction and murders of Andre Lang's wife and daughter. The similarities to Dana Bradford's murder were scary to say the least. His next move was to speak to the investigator who had handled the case to get his take on things before he hauled Andre in for questioning.

"Moore speaking," David Moore, twenty-year, veteran of the Memphis Police Department answered in his distinctive Tennessean twang.

"Afternoon, detective," Keith replied. "This is Detective Keith Wilson with the Atlanta police department. How are you today, sir?"

"Pretty good. Keepin Busy. Never too busy to help the folks down in Atlanta though. Whatcha got?"

"According to records, you worked a real nasty homicide about three years ago involving a doctor whose wife and daughter mysteriously vanished, then turned up butchered three days later. Ring any bells?"

"'Course," Moore replied. "You don't forget a case like that, son." He couldn't wait to recount the tale of Dr. Lang that had no doubt become infamous amongst Memphis law enforcement circles. "Why are you interested in that case?"

"A young woman was found, raped and murdered in the exact same way here in Atlanta a couple months back. Turns out Lang may have been her gynecologist."

"God almighty. Lang a suspect?"

"Not officially."

"Well, good luck, son. Let me know how I can help in anyway."

"Thanks."

"So, Dr. Lang is in Atlanta, huh? And he's resumed his practice?" Moore asked, seemingly perplexed.

"Which part has you more confused," Keith inquired. "The fact that he moved, or the fact that he resumed his profession?"

"Well, I'm sure that I don't have to tell you that the way those poor gals were killed can easily be seen as being done by some sort of whacked out anti-abortion radical. We never could prove it, but that didn't stop Dr. Lang from being overcome with guilt 'cause of his profession, you know. He vowed that he would never perform an abortion again."

"I see," Keith said, then went straight to the true point of his call. "Was Lang ever a suspect?"

"'Course, Detective. Husband is always the initial suspect in a murder case like that. We had search warrants, checked his emails, bank accounts, social media, and all that. Everything came up empty."

Keith knew that was standard procedure, but that was not what he asked. A detective, especially a veteran like Detective Moore, develops a kind of gut instincts that nags at him, letting him know if a suspect is guilty or not.

"In your opinion," he asked slowly. "Between me and you and the lamp post, what do *you* think happened to Rene and Zhuri Lang?"

"If you're askin' do I think that Dr. Lang went psycho one night on his family, the answer is…" Keith held his breath. "No, Detective Wilson. I never believed for a second that Andre Lang had anything to do with that."

Just as Keith was just about to breathe a sigh of relief because at least Mackenzie wasn't involved with a psychotic killer who had gotten away with murder, Detective Moore added, "'Course there were others who felt differently."

"What do you mean?" Keith asked.

"I mean my partner felt that Lang had somethin' to do with it, at first. He had a hard on about it for a long time."

Keith looked through the case file. "Detective Turner, right? I probably should reach out to him, too. Get his take on things."

"You could if he were still alive," Moore said. "But I honestly don't think Lang had anything to do with it."

We'll see. "Thanks for your time detective."

———————

Andre pressed his hands against Mackenzie's stone-tiled shower wall. Water cascaded like warm rain down his face, mixing with the remnants of his tears. He closed his eyes, letting in more images of Rene and Zhuri. He thought about the conversation he needed to have with Mackenzie about what had really happened to his family. Tell her the stupid reason he had lied to her and the frightening similarities to Dana Bradford's murder. It was all too much to handle. She would probably run at warp speed to get away from him and any danger he could bring into her life. To her children. He could not blame her.

Andre stepped out of the shower, dried off, then used the towel to wipe the foggy vanity mirror until his bloodshot eyes came into view. *You really fucked up.* He wrapped the towel around his waist before walking into Mackenzie's bedroom. She was laying in the bed on her stomach talking on the phone. Bright afternoon sunlight filtered through cracks in the drapes, caressing her naked body.

"I haven't really thought about it," she said to whoever she was speaking. She looked up at him, covering her hand over the phone. "It's my mother," she whispered to him, playfully rolling her eyes. Andre nodded then sat on the edge of the bed. Mackenzie continued the call. "I'm pretty sure Nate and Beverly will do it big as usual. You know Beverly," she said. "Yeah, the kids would love to see y'all. OK. Call Nate to see what he has planned. Yes, mama. Love you. Tell daddy I love him too. Bye." She hung up, then wrapped her arms around his waste from behind. "My mom is planning for her and my dad to come up for Thanksgiving."

"That's nice," he said, feigning a smile.

"What are you doing for Thanksgiving, baby?" she asked, rubbing his back.

"I haven't thought about it," he said dryly. He had not celebrated any holiday in years. Thanksgiving was especially avoided more than a pit of venomous snakes. Sadly, this year would turn out no different.

"You're welcome to join us. My mother and Beverly will probably get on your nerves, but between the two of them at least the food will be to-go plate worthy. Mama's seafood dressing is legendary." She chuckled. "At least that's what she loves to remind us. Joel should bring Ethan, too."

Andre looked back to meet the love in her smiling eyes. Anxious. Preparing to tell her the truth. His cell phone vibrated on the nightstand. It was Mrs. Lopez, one of his patients. Andre was slightly relieved for the interruption.

"One second, baby," he said, answering the call. Mrs. Lopez told him that she was having contractions and that she was taking a taxi to the hospital since her husband was out of town on business. "OK. I'll meet you there."

"Everything, OK?" Mackenzie asked.

"Yeah. One of my patients might be in labor, so I need to get over to the hospital," he said, standing.

Mackenzie watched him slide into his clothes. There was something off about him. His forehead was furrowed and the glow he usually radiated was faint. "Are you alright?"

He leaned in to kiss her as he buttoned his shirt. "I'm fine, baby. Just a little tired," he lied.

"Tired?" she chuckled, wrapping herself in her duvet. "We can't have that. I'll be ready for another round when you get back so pick up some Redbulls."

Andre grabbed his car keys from the nightstand. "I'll call you when I'm done," he said.

Fucked up.

"Yes, sir she had a breeched birth," Andre said to Mrs. Lopez's husband over the phone. Andre could tell from his labored breathing and din in the background that he was rushing through an airport terminal. "I had to perform an emergency C-section, but both your baby girl and your wife are fine. They are resting comfortably at the hospital. You're very welcome, Mr. Lopez. Safe travels."

Andre hung up to text Mackenzie that he was on his way back. The doorbell rang in unison with him hitting send, startling him. He turned to view the surveillance video of the unexpected visitor. Standing at the door was Mackenzie's friend, Detective Keith Wilson.

Andre went to open the office door. "What's going on?" he asked, looking around the parking lot. He knew why Keith had showed up.

"We need to talk, man." Keith pushed past Andre, quickly scanning the waiting area with the eyes of a seasoned investigator.

"Why are you here, man?"

Keith turned to him. *Mackenzie is really into this lame ass pretty boy?* "Dana Bradford," he said bluntly. "She was found murdered in Piedmont Park in the exact same way that your wife and daughter were killed in Memphis. That couldn't be a simple coincidence."

Andre slowly shook his head. "No, it couldn't be," he sighed, leaning back against the receptionist desk.

Keith raised his left eyebrow. "The details of her death were not made public, but you don't seem surprised."

"Mackenzie was worried about you last night. She mentioned that you told her the details. But, just as the police in Memphis concluded and like I'm telling you now: I had nothing to do with their murders."

Keith looked at Andre directly in the eyes for any secrets that his soul hid. "I didn't say you did. I just want to know how Dana came into possession of this." He handed Andre a magazine from the manila folder that he was carrying. "And what was you're connection to her."

It was a copy of *Elle*. Kerry Washington was on the cover striking a sexy pose. Andre noticed the mailing label was addressed to him at his practice. "I have no idea how she got this," he said after a moment, returning the magazine to Keith. "There are plenty of similar magazines in this waiting room. Anyone could have taken it."

Keith glanced in the direction of magazines on the coffee table. "Yeah, I get that," he said. "You perform abortions here, right? Dana had an abortion a couple week before she was murdered. Was she one of your patients?"

"No. I haven't performed an abortion in several years. And Dana Bradford was not one of my patients."

"How can you be sure?"

"Because I run a small practice. I have a personal relationship with all of my patients."

Keith produced a picture from the folder. "Ever meet her?" he asked, holding it up to Andre's face.

Andre took the picture. It was of the young blonde girl smiling in a skimpy red bikini on a sunny beach. He couldn't place her face, but her features reminded him of someone he may have met in passing. He covered her eyes with his hand. *Cindy Myers.* The young lady that had come in inquiring about having an abortion a few months back.

"I think I know who she is," he said.

CHAPTER 20

"Later guys." Traci waved to her friends as they exited school, which was more like a ghost town today. She felt accomplished having braved four intense weekends of pre-SAT study groups. Thanks to her preparation acing the test was a sure thing. Traci sat outside on a bench. A breeze foreshadowing rain rustled through the red leaf maple trees. The school band was rehearsing Cardi B's *Bodak Yellow* in the distance. Traci turned on her phone to text her mom and request an Uber to her uncle Nate's house.

"What up, bae?" Antonio said, walking towards her. He wore his favorite hoodie covering his head.

"Hey," she beamed. "How was practice?"

"Dope. My three-pointer is a beast." He showed off his moves, somehow landing face-up on Traci's lap. "People gon' be sayin', Kobe? Lebron? Who? It's all about that Antonio Osborne."

"That's right, bae." Traci giggled.

"How was study group?"

"Long, but worth it. I should do well on the test."

"Of course, you will," Antonio said, sitting up. "We gonna be the next Barack and Michelle."

"Yeah, but you need to put the basketball down sometimes and prepare for the SAT, too. We can't be Barack and Michelle if you don't get into a good college."

"I don't have to worry about that. You know. I'm going to get a scholarship to a good school. Division one. And then, I am heading to the NBA."

"What if you don't?"

"That's why I got my sexy, beautiful, genius to tutor me." He pressed his forehead to hers. "I drove today. Let's go study at my house. My folks aren't home."

Traci pulled back, sure that if she went with him, studying would not be the only thing they did—if they studied at all. "'Tonio. You know I can't do that. My mom would kill me."

"Come on, bae." Antonio begged, planting soft kisses on her neck. "I really just wanna study, bae. I promise."

Traci could see the outline of Antonio's hard dick poking through his grey sweat pants. The manly scent of the Gucci cologne she had bought him, his hypnotizing bedroom eyes, and devilish smile made her panties wet. She missed making love to him and being wrapped in his strong arms.

A black sedan pulled up.

"Traci?" the driver shouted.

Traci jumped up, relieved to be saved from temptation. "My Uber's here. Call you when I get home," she said. "Love you."

"Love you too, bae." Antonio waved, watching the car speed away.

"How may I help you?" Joel answered the phone like Mackenzie was interrupting him. He was combing through his closet for something stylish but casual to wear.

"Ethan must be over there giving you some 'cause you're being extra," Mackenzie said. She lay back across her bed with a bowl of grapes.

"Yeah, he's in the shower," Joel said with a satisfied grin on his face. "We're about to fight the lines at Atlantic Station to go ice skating."

"Aww, that's cute. You're actually dating someone instead of being the usual man-whore."

"Whatever, bitch." Joel said. "Shouldn't you be cuddled up with the good doctor?"

"He had to go to the hospital for a delivery. The kids are still at Nate's for the weekend, so you're my entertainment for a while."

"Yay, me," he said dryly. "Glad you're finally putting those rusty old pipes of yours to good use."

"Please. This cat is so wet, it sounds like someone stirring good mac and cheese when Andre is diggin' up in it." She made squishing sounds for emphasis. "Creamy, gushy magic."

Joel burst out laughing. "I just threw up in my mouth. You're traumatizing me."

"You brought it up," she said, popping a grape into her mouth. "Speaking of mac and cheese. What are you doing for Thanksgiving."

"I have no clue," he said, holding up an outdated sweater, grimacing as he tossed it in a pile of rejects on the floor.

"Good. My parents are coming up. We're having dinner at Nate and Beverly's house. I'm bringing Andre. You and Ethan can come too, if he's free, or you haven't dumped him by then."

"Sounds tempting. I love your mama's cooking and the shade between her and Beverly over who makes the best dressing or greens will be a good show."

"Actually, I think I'll make the dressing this year. We all know my mine is the best."

"First of all, no one knows that. And if you bring Andre be prepared to run him off with that concoction of Styrofoam and chalk mixed with oysters that you call dressing. So, let your mama or Beverly handle it. Your cooch ain't that magical."

Mackenzie chuckled. Her phone line beeped before she could defend her cooking skills. "Hold on. Nate's calling. The twins are probably doing something they've got no business doing."

"OK."

"Hey, big bro," she answered. "What did they do now?"

"Mackenzie, is Traci supposed to be coming over today," Nate asked.

Mackenzie sat up. "Yeah. She texted me that she's taking an Uber to you right after study group. Why?"

"She texted me too, but she never showed."

Mackenzie scrolled through her messages. Traci's last text was over a thirty minutes ago. She should have already made it to Nate's by now. Mackenzie's heart rate shot up. "Did you try calling her?"

"Yeah. My calls keep going straight to voicemail. And no response from my texts," Nate said."

"Let me call you back." Mackenzie hung up to call Antonio's mother. Traci wasn't supposed to be with Antonio, but her being with him was far better than the alternative. She forgot that Joel was still on the line.

"I was just about to hang up," he said.

"Joel have you talked to Traci today?"

"No. Why?"

178

"She was supposed to Uber to Nate's after school. Nate said she never showed, and her phone keeps going to voicemail."

———————

Ethan stepped into Joel's bedroom nude and grinning while drying himself off. The sleeve of tattoos snaking along his left arm to his chest accentuated his sexiness.

"Your shower head is magical," Ethan said. "Where—" He stopped in mid-sentence. Joel was sitting on the bed mumbling to himself, focused on sending a text. The worried look on Joel's face told Ethan that something was wrong.

"Come on Traci don't do this to your mom," Joel whispered. "Where are you?"

"Everything OK, babe?" Ethan asked.

Joel looked up. "Mackenzie's daughter is missing. Her phone keeps going to voicemail."

Ethan wrapped the towel around his waist. He sat next to Joel. "Missing? What do you mean?"

"She texted Mackenzie that she was taking an Uber to Mackenzie's brother's house after school. She didn't show up. That's the last they heard from her."

"Shit. Did Mackenzie call the police yet?"

Joel stood up. "I don't know but I'm going over there."

———————

Mackenzie's pacing burned a hole in her kitchen floor. Antonio's mother wasn't answering the phone fast enough. Anxiety swarmed her mind more than a hive of angry bees. *Please answer.* She imagined that she heard a million rings before Cynthia finally answered.

"Hello."

"Cynthia it's Mackenzie, Traci's mother," she blurted out.

"Hey, Mackenzie."

"Is Antonio home?"

"He should be, but we aren't there. What's wrong?"

"I can't find Traci. Do you know if Antonio saw her today?"

"Oh my God. I'll ask him. Hold on." The line went silent. Cynthia clicked over to call Antonio. "Antonio," Cynthia said when the phone lines merged. Mackenzie listened ready to jump in.

"Hey, ma." Antonio said.

"Where are you?"

"At the house."

"Is Traci over there with you?" Cynthia grilled him. "Please don't lie, son. You won't get in trouble."

"No."

Mackenzie interrupted. "Antonio, this is Traci's mother. When did you last see her?"

Antonio hesitated, wondering if this was about him asking Traci to sneak home with him. "I saw her after practice today right before she got in an Uber," he said.

Mackenzie's heart froze. She couldn't breathe.

CHAPTER 21

Andre entered Mackenzie's house using a spare key. On the way over, he had prepared himself for the conversation they needed to have. His encounter with Keith was still stinging behind his eyes. Andre was sure that the young lady in the picture Keith had showed him was Cindy Myers; the same girl that had come to the office a few months back requesting an abortion.

He had showed Keith security footage from the office on the day of Cindy's visit. Keith concluded that Cindy was really Dana Bradford hiding under a hat and dark shades. When Rene and Zhuri were killed the Memphis, police had theorized that it was done by anti-abortion extremist. Dana being murdered in the exact same way made their theory more like a fact.

Mackenzie was in the kitchen on the phone. Her bloodshot eyes showed that she had been crying.

"She's African American, about five feet six and one hundred fifteen pounds. She's got hazel eyes and shoulder length hair,"

Makenzie said, cupping her forehead. She paused as if she were being asked a question. "I don't know what she was wearing. She's staying with my brother for the weekend." Andre stood in front of her, ready to assist with whatever was happening. "Her friend said that he saw her get into a black car about thirty minutes ago. I logged into the Uber app. It says the ride she requested was cancelled and the car was red not black." After a few minutes, Mackenzie rattled off her phone number and address. She dropped the phone on the kitchen counter, then collapsed into Andre's arms.

"What's happening Mackenzie?"

"Traci's missing." She could barely get the words out. "The police are on their way."

Andre's eyes nearly popped out of their sockets. *This can't be happening again.*

Keith battled slow traffic along the wet highway. Puddles of rain splashed on his windshield. An ambulance roared past on its way to a yet another car accident. Keith was lulled by the steady tempo of his windshield wipers. Kendrick Lamar *Humble* was on the radio. He thought about the connection between the murders of Andre's wife, daughter and Dana Bradford. In his many years of law enforcement, Keith had learned that there was no such thing as a coincidence. Now Mackenzie was caught up in this mess. Keith was determined to protect her.

He had left his confrontation with Andre with mixed feelings. Keith did not believe that Andre had murdered his family, but Andre not telling Mackenzie about it did not sit well with him. Keith decided to give him the courtesy to tell Mackenzie today before he told her all that was happening. His cell rang. It was Mackenzie. Keith put the call on Bluetooth.

"Hey, Mackenzie," Keith answered, expecting her to relay what Andre had told her.

"Keith, I need your help," she said.

"What's wrong?"

"My daughter's missing. The police are on their way, but is there anything you can do to help?"

Shit. Keith maneuvered to exit the highway as fast as he could. "I'm on my way."

———————

Mackenzie hung up with Keith. She wiped away the tears blurring her vision and braced herself on the kitchen counter. She couldn't stop imagining Traci scared and crying out for her. Recent news reports about young girls being abducted into sex trafficking rings and worst added to her fears. "Traci is OK," she said to stop a panic attack as best she could. "This is just a misunderstanding, but she is OK."

Andre came up behind her, feeling her pain, hoping that he was not the cause of it. He prayed that everything would work out. He couldn't live with himself if it did not. It was all too familiar.

He gently placed his hands on her shoulders. "Mackenzie, I need to tell you something."

Mackenzie turned to face him. Before Andre could speak the doorbell rang.

"That must be the police," she said, rushing to answer the door. Andre followed. Standing on the other side was a female uniformed Atlanta police officer, a stone expression on her face. Mackenzie couldn't decipher whether or not she recognized the seriousness.

"Mrs. Hill?" the officer asked.

"Yes."

"You called about your daughter. I'm here to do a report. May I come in?"

Mackenzie stepped aside. "Please."

Mackenzie led her to living room. One of the first questions she asked was did Traci have any reason to run away.

Mackenzie was insulted. "My child has no reason to run away."

Andre stepped in. "This might have something to do with me."

Mackenzie turned to him. She was confused. "What do you mean?"

"This seems like what happened to my wife and daughter. That's what I wanted to tell you. Something horrible may be going on."

"What? You told me that your family was killed in a fire."

"I wasn't being honest," Andre said. "They were murdered."

———————

Joel sped to Mackenzie's house as fast as he could, almost blowing through a stop sign. The rain had stopped but damage to the already skittish traffic was done. Luckily, he had been to Mackenzie's house so many times that every shortcut was second nature.

He parked in the driveway behind Andre's SUV. Traci's phone was still going straight to voicemail and Mackenzie not answering gave him a bad feeling. The sight of an Atlanta PD cruiser sitting outside of Mackenzie's house made it worst. Joel quickly walked inside. A female police officer was talking to Andre. Mackenzie was sitting on her couch with her hands clasped and crying. She stood to hug Joel when she saw him.

He braced for bad news. "What's going on?"

"I don't know," she said, sounding defeated. "Traci's phone is still off. Antonio saw her get into a black car after school, but it wasn't the Uber she requested."

Fuck! "Did the police put out an Amber alert?"

"They just did and they are going try to use Find My iPhone app, check her email and social media," she said. "Interview Antonio, too."

"Good." He noticed Mackenzie struggling to compose herself. Seeing his best friend like that made him tear up. He sat down next to her. "Everything will work out Z. I know it will."

She shook her head as a new batch of tears flowed. "You haven't heard the worst of it."

"Worst?"

"Andre didn't tell me his wife and daughter were murdered."

"Wait. Murdered? I thought that they died in a fire."

"I did, too. I just found out that they were murdered in the same horrible way that Dana Bradford was killed. Dana was a patient of Andre. He thinks that there may be a connection."

Joel was dumbstruck. He was about to ask Mackenzie for more details when the cop came up to them.

"Mrs. Hill," she said. Mackenzie looked up. "We have all the information from Dr. Lang. Antonio Osborne gave a description of the vehicle and driver. An APB has been put out for the car and an Amber alert has been issued."

Joel jumped up. "What's next?" he asked.

The cop barely acknowledged Joel. "We're doing all we can to find her, sir. Most times it really is as simple as a resentful teenager running away."

"What hell does that mean?" Joel exploded. "Traci's not the type of girl to run away. And you're standing here acting like she is just another delinquent black teenager when you know Andre's story. Time is not on our side."

The cop turned to Joel. "Sir, I understand your frustration, but I assure you that all of our resources are in motion. I'm a mother, too. I take this very seriously."

Andre stepped in. "I've heard this kind of dismissive talk before. Please understand that our fear is justified."

The cop was about to respond to Andre when Joel cut in. "Stop acting like you're some kind shining white knight. This is your fault. Why did you lie to Mackenzie?"

Joel's condemning words cut through Andre like a hot knife through butter. He didn't know what to say.

CHAPTER 22

She walked up on to the back porch of the dilapidated house, the pungent stench of urine competing with a stray dog's loud barking. Police sirens wailed in the distance. She jumped to avoid cockroaches that were scampering around. *I hate coming over here,* she frowned, pulling strands of spiderwebs from her hair. She knocked on the door. After a minute it creaked open.

"About fuckin' time you got here," he said, leaning shirtless in the doorway, puffing on a cigarette.

"You know I don't like coming to this nasty dump," she said, looking around in disgust; her face puckered like she had just eaten a lemon. "What's so important that you had to see me?"

He moved to the side and pointed. Blindfolded, gagged with duct tape and tied to the filthy mattress was a young girl.

"Change of plans," he smirked, blowing smoke in her face.

Keith rang Mackenzie's doorbell. Driving up to her house, he saw Andre's Range Rover parked in the driveway, a red BMW parked behind it. He thought about Dana Branford's murder, the possible connection to Andre, and now Mackenzie's daughter being missing. He prayed that things were not as they seemed.

The door opened. Mackenzie's friend Joel was standing on the other side.

"Hey, man." he said, shaking Joel's hand. Keith had not seen Joel since the night they briefly met while he was on the date with Mackenzie. Since the night he had insulted him. He still felt stupid. "Mackenzie here?"

"Yeah, she's in the kitchen talking to Andre." He pointed towards the living room. You can have a seat if you like. I'll go get her."

"Thanks."

Joel went to the kitchen. Keith chose to stand in the foyer. Under different circumstances, he would have loved to be in Mackenzie's house, sitting on her sofa where she had sat, smelling her lingering perfume in the air. Now, he hated that he had to be here.

Mackenzie sat at the kitchen table across from Andre. She massaged her temples to keep her brain from bursting out of her skull. Andre was trying to explain why he did not tell her how his wife and child were really killed. His lips were moving, his words may have even been sincere. Mackenzie was too fatigued with anxiety about bringing Traci home safe to care.

"I wanted to tell you when we first met," Andre said his head lower than a puppy who got caught shitting on the carpet. "When I've tried telling women in the past they usually ended up treating me like I'm damaged goods if they stuck around. Maybe I am, but I didn't want that for us."

"I don't want to talk about this right now," Mackenzie said barely audible.

Andre kept talking as if he didn't hear her.

"Damn it, Andre. I said, I don't want to talk about this right now," she slammed her hands on the table just as Joel came into the kitchen.

"Keith is here," Joel said.

Mackenzie bolted to Keith. Hopefully he had some answers. Andre and Joel followed her.

Keith watched Mackenzie rushing toward him. Joel and Andre were close behind. If pain were a person, it would be wearing a Mackenzie costume.

"Keith," she said. "Have you heard anything?"

Keith hated having to dampen her hopes. On the way over he had made some calls to try to find out any updates. Sadly, there were none.

"Not yet." He sighed. "But I have my partner helping and the initial contact officer has given me all Traci's information." Mackenzie looked defeated. "We will find her, Mackenzie."

Andre was leaning against the wall, looking remorseful. "What can I do to help?" he asked Keith. Keith ignored him. "What can I do to help?"

Keith let the anger grenade that he held inside detonate. He charged straight up to Andre, almost punching him in the face. "What you should have done is told Mackenzie the truth from the get go," he said through gritted teeth, his finger pointed in Andre's head.

"Let her decide if she wanted to deal with your baggage, instead of lying like a little bitch."

Andre noticed Keith's tightly balled fist. He pushed him away. "Either you swing or get the fuck out of my face, man. You think that I don't know that? That I don't hate this?"

"That's not good enough."

"Stop it." Mackenzie demanded, watching them size each up other like a pair of territorial lions.

Joel got between Keith and Andre. "Are ya'll crazy? Do you think we need this shit right now?"

Keith backed away, realizing that he was only adding to Mackenzie's stress. He turned to her. "I'm so sorry," he said. "I should probably go, but please know that I am on top of this. I will call you with any updates."

"Thank you," Mackenzie said.

"You're welcome," he said, leaving through the door.

Andre went to embrace Mackenzie, but she blocked him.

"I think you should go, too."

"Mackenzie, I don't want to leave you alone."

She pointed at Joel. "I'm not alone. Joel's here and my brother will be over soon."

Andre continued to plead his case. "Mackenzie please just listen." She walked away with outlooking back. He started to follow her.

Joel stepped in front of him, shoving him in the chest.

"Just leave, man," Joel said. "She'll call you later."

Andre watched Mackenzie go upstairs. He turned to leave. *What have I done?*

CHAPTER 23

Antonio slumped on the couch with angry tears filling his eyes as he watched his parents show Detective Parnell out the front door. Antonio had just finished answering questions about the last time that he had seen Traci. Did he see anyone suspicious? How she had been acting? His relationship with her? Was she being bullied at school. Anything little he could think of that would be helpful in finding her. He couldn't believe what was happening. He sprang from the couch and ran up to his room.

"Antonio!" his mother called after him. His father pulled at her.

"Just let him go, Cynt. The boy probably just wants to be alone right now." She snatched away from him to chase after her child.

"Antonio," she said, bursting into his room. Antonio was ripping down the posters of basketball players from his walls.

Cynthia teared up. "Baby, stop," she said calmly, reaching out to console him. He dodged her and snatched up his book bag from the bed.

"It's my fault. If I wasn't trying to get in her pants, she would have known that car wasn't her Uber. I'm going to go find her myself." He raced down the stairs, straight into his father's arms.

"Whoa. Where are you going, son?"

"Let me go, dad." Antonio tried to push past him. He may have been taller, but there was no use trying to get pass the brick wall that was Harold Osborne. "Let me go. I need to help her."

He felt helpless seeing his son wheezing and letting out snotty tears—the kind he hadn't seen since Antonio was small when he fell off his bike or twisted his ankle on the basketball court. "Calm down, son" he said, hugging him tight as he looked at his wife. "Everything will be OK."

———

Traci's eyes slowly flickered back to consciousness. She had no idea what was happening. Wherever she was had no light or sound. Just the nasty smell of cigarettes mixed with mold. She tried to scream for help, but her mouth was sealed shut with duct tape. Restraints on her arms and legs held her down. She felt sick with panic, chocking on tears as she struggled to break free.

Mom. Dad. Please, help me!

A florescent light snapped on in the room, revealing a man standing over her. The sinister look on his face sent tremors through Traci's body.

"Wakey, wakey little one," the killer said, grinning.

———

The sun was beginning to cast a bizarre shade of orange against the purplish sky. Precious hours had passed since Mackenzie had called Keith. He had finished looking around Traci's school parking lot for any clue to her abduction that may have been missed. Maybe an ATM security camera pointed at the school that he needed to check out. Or a handwritten note from Traci, pleading for help that was thrown on the ground. Anything since dispatch had confirmed that this was the last ping of Traci's cell phone. Her phone was off, so tracking wasn't possible.

Parnell walked up to him. He had sent Parnell over to question her boyfriend. The look on his face was not a good sign.

"Please tell me the boyfriend told you something," Keith asked.

"Sorry, man. He is just a kid that has the hots for his girlfriend, posting pictures of the two of them all over IG."

Keith wasn't surprised. Still, he was not about to give up until he had kicked over ever rock. Time was quickly winding down. His phone rang. It was Mackenzie. His stomach knotted, knowing the lack of news that he was about to deliver. "Hey, Mackenzie," he said. "No. Nothing has come up yet, but I promise you that I will not give up." He was quiet, listening to her speak. "No problem. Call me as often as you need." Mackenzie hung up. Keith slammed his fist on his car roof. *Fuck!*

"What's the next move?" Parnell asked.

"I want to question Andre, again."

———————

Big brothers are supposed to protect their little sisters. Help fix their problems, right down to beating up cheating boyfriends. That's how Nate had always been with Mackenzie, especially after Marlon had died. Now he didn't know how to help. Truthfully, he was freaking out himself, imagining his niece in this frightening situation. What would he do if this was happened to any of his kids?

Mackenzie hung up the phone with Keith. She burst out crying. A cold ache shot from her stomach to every part of her body.

"I don't know what to do, Nate. I don't know what to do."

Nate squeezed his sister tightly, holding back his own tears. Joel came into the bedroom with a glass of water and two Valiums that Mackenzie had left over from when Marlon died. He handed them to Nate.

"Thanks, man." Nate said. Joel went back downstairs. "Here. Take these, sis."

Mackenzie pushed his hand away. "I don't want to be sedated, Nate. I need to be ready for anything. Keith could be calling back any minute."

"Right. And when he does, I will be right here to hear the good news. So, will Joel. I promise."

"Nate. I've let Traci down too many times before. I can't do it again. Especially not this time. That's my child."

"And she is my niece and you're my little sister having a nervous breakdown. Traci needs for us to be level headed right now." Mackenzie's empty expression showed that she wasn't listening. "If you don't take these I'm calling mom," he said.

Mackenzie snapped back to life. She snatched the pills out of his hand. "I'd rather take the damn valium."

———

The last time Ethan had seen Andre like this was when Rene and Zhuri were missing. Overwhelmed with fear and anger. The guilt of being alive when he wished that he was dead. This time Andre was far worst. He blamed himself for what was happening to Mackenzie and her daughter. For what he had brought into her life. No question,

Ethan would be there for his friend, but he wasn't so sure that Andre was wrong.

"Any word, bro?" Ethan asked Andre, sitting next to him on Joel's couch.

"No. I've tried calling and texting but no response."

"Give her time."

Andre shook his head at the word *time*. "Time is what kills. I can't just sit here doing nothing."

"I have to ask you, bro. As your friend. Even as a lawyer. Why didn't you tell Mackenzie how Rene and Zhuri were really killed?"

"Because I'm selfish."

"You're a lot of things. I wouldn't call you selfish."

"If you say so." Andre sighed. "Losing Rene and Zhuri ripped my heart out. I'll never be completely over it, but I guess I just wanted a fresh start with Mackenzie without the baggage. My therapist warned me that I was moving too fast. I should have listened."

"I can understand you wanting a fresh start. You've been through some heavy shit."

"When Mackenzie told me that Dana was killed the same way that they were, and Keith found out that Dana had even been to my office, I should have told Mackenzie right away. It can't be a coincidence."

"You don't know that," Ethan said. "We don't even know if what happening to Traci has anything to do with you."

"Thanks, bro, but you know that it does."

Ethan's phone rang. It was Joel calling. Ethan quickly answered.

"Hey, Joel," Ethan said. "Any news?" Andre's ears perked up.

———

Nate sat in the kitchen with Joel waiting for any news. Joel's phone conversation with his boyfriend was laced with worry in his voice and etched on his face. Nate had first met Joel through Mackenzie so long ago that Joel had become more than a friend, he was part of the family. Nate appreciated that Joel was always there for his sister and her kids.

Nate motioned to Joel that he was going to check on Mackenzie.

Joel nodded. A moment later heard two short knocks at the door. "Hold on. Someone's at the door," he said to Ethan, rushing to answer it. Standing on the porch was tall white man, wearing a grey hoodie that covered the upper half of his face. "Yes?"

The man lowered his hood. "I'm here to see Mackenzie Hill," he said. His voice sounded like he was eating molasses.

Joel was struck by the cold behind his piercing, steel grey eyes. This person was not there to deliver any sort of good news.

"Is Traci, OK?"

He slowly shook his head. "No," he replied. "I'm afraid not. May I come inside?"

"No. Not Traci." Joel said, his voice barely above a whisper. He didn't want Mackenzie or Nate to hear any bad news just yet. "What happened to her?"

The man stepped inside the foyer, quickly shutting the door behind him. "Don't worry. You'll find out soon."

Faster than Joel could process it, he whipped out his hunting knife, and slashed Joel deep along the left side of his neck. Joel stumbled backwards, clutching the wound, blood gushing from the spaces between his fingers. He sucked in a breath to scream for help. All he could produce was a squeak and more blood from his shredded vocal chords. Seconds hovered between living and dying. Joel swung as hard as he could and his right fist connected with the man's jaw. He grabbed a glass vase from the credenza smashing it against his skull. He was not about to go down without a fight or let this monster hurt Mackenzie.

The man shrugged off Joel like a hyena toying with injured prey. He delighted in seeing Joel struggle, his strength fading, wheezing for his last breaths of life. With a final blow, he plunged his blade into Joel's stomach all the way to the hilt. Joel dropped to his knees, still clinging to the man's hoodie. His adrenaline surge drained out of him faster than water down a flushed toilet. He had no more fight to give. He collapsed face down, his eyes opened but seeing only darkness, blood pooling beneath his body.

Mackenzie was lying across her bed, staring at her phone as if she could will it to ring with good news from the police or Traci.

"How you feeling, sis?" Nate asked.

Mackenzie sat up. "The valium helped calm me a little I guess, but I won't feel real peace until Traci is home safe."

"Me either," Nate said. "Beverly sends her love and prayers. She said the twins are behaving."

"Thanks."

"That's what big brothers are here for. What do we tell mom and dad?"

Mackenzie's face scrunched up in confusion. Why he would Nate suggest telling their parents? They both knew how their mother would react. Calls would come every five seconds. She would blame Mackenzie, upset their father and force him drive to Atlanta before they knew all the facts. "Not right now," she said sternly. "Let's just work on bringing Traci home before she comes up to drain me even more."

The sound of breaking glass resonated through the house. Mackenzie and Nate looked at each other.

"Probably just Joel being clumsy," Mackenzie said.

"I'll check."

Downstairs all the lights were off. Nate senses warned him that something wasn't right. "You OK, man?" he called out, fumbling along the wall until he found the light switch. The light revealed the disturbing sight of Joel lying face down on the floor, blood seeping from his neck, mixed with shards of glass. He immediately rushed over to help him.

"So, you must be the big brother," Nate heard someone say. He turned to see a man scrapping a bloody knife on his jeans. "Nice to meet you."

CHAPTER 24

"Joel, Joel." Ethan shouted at the phone, hearing the scuffling in the background, followed by silence.

"What's wrong?" Andre asked.

"I don't know," Ethan said. "I heard something, then the call dropped." He redialed Joel's number. Joel didn't answer. Ethan dialed again. Still no answer. "We should call the police and go over there."

Andre had his phone out to call Mackenzie. She didn't answer either. He dialed 911, giving them all the information and Mackenzie' address.

"Let's go," he said after he hung up. As they were about to rush out the door, Andre's phone rang. He didn't recognize the number. "Hello."

"Andre, this is detective Wilson."

"Detective," Andre said, looking at Ethan, both of their hearts pounding. "What's going on?"

"I need to talk to you again," Keith said.

"What's going on at Mackenzie's house?"

"What do you mean?"

"You need to get over there ASAP."

Nate quickly accessed the threat looming in front of him. He knew that he had only seconds to act, knife or no knife. "Mackenzie call the police," he shouted upstairs. His former football playing skills kicked it. He tackled the man, wrestling the knife from his hand and body slammed him against the hard floor.

"Where the fuck is my niece?" Nate demanded. He pinned the man's chest down with his knees, pounding him with heavy punches to the face. "Where is she, you piece of shit?"

He only laughed, getting some sort of sick pleasure from Nate's anger. He coughed up the cooper tasting blood covering his face.

"Guess."

Hearing Nate's frantic commands, Mackenzie charged down the stairs, still on the phone with 911. The horror that she saw stopped her momentum and caused her to drop her phone. "Joel." Mackenzie screamed so loud that she burst her own eardrums. The shock of seeing Joel sprawled face down in a pool of blood rendered her numb.

Nate hearing Mackenzie's screams was enough of a distraction for the man to reach the knife that was lying a few inches from his hand. He slashed Nate on his side. Nate doubled over in pain. As the man went in for the kill, Mackenzie picked up the first thing she saw that would have maximum impact. She ran up behind him and bashed him over the head with a heavy elephant sculpture.

He jumped up. "That hurt bitch." He yanked Mackenzie by her hair and shoved the knife against her throat. "Don't you want to see your brat again?"

Nate tried to stand. "Let my sister go."

The man kicked Nate in the face. "Shut the fuck up."

———————

Keith and Parnell nearly fishtailed driving up to Mackenzie house. They saw the flashing squad car lights and yellow police tape outside. Two EMT's rushed Joel out on a stretcher. An oxygen mask was covering his face and his white shirt was stained bright red. They loaded him in an ambulance that speed away, sirens roaring.

Keith was shocked by the amount of blood on Mackenzie's foyer floor and spattered on the walls. Her living room was trashed from a scuffle. He went up to Nate, who was being questioned by a uniformed officer. His torso was wrapped with bandages, but Nate had refused to be taken to the hospital. He insisted that they let him go so that he could help find Mackenzie instead.

"What happened?" he asked Nate. "Where is Mackenzie?"

Nate whipped around to Keith, grimacing in pain from the stab wound. "Some piece of shit took her."

"Shit." Keith said to Parnell.

———————

Mackenzie lay stiff in the trunk of a car. Her arms and legs bound. Her head covered with a greasy towel. She had no idea where she was being taken. All she knew was that this person had said that she had better come with him if she wanted Traci back alive. She had a silent meltdown picturing Joel sprawled out on the ground. She couldn't believe that the laughter and love they had shared spanning twenty years were gone. Mackenzie closed her eyes and said a prayer for Joel just as the car hard braked to a stop.

The trunk popped open and the man leaned over her.

"Showtime," he said.

Andre and Ethan turned on Mackenzie's street. The sight of two police cars in front of her house sent tremors through Andre. *What had he done?* He jumped out of the car, sprinting up to the door. A police officer denied him access to the active crime scene.

"Mackenzie," he yelled through the open door. "Mackenzie."

Keith was in the living room gathering more information from Nate. He heard Andre and came outside.

"The fuck you doing here?" Keith frowned.

"Where is Mackenzie, man?" Andre demanded.

Rage boiled over in Keith. He shot out on to the lawn, his fist connecting to Andre's jaw with a definitive crack. Andre charged at him, sending them both tumbling to the ground. They came up together on their knees, ready to exchange blows. Parnell and the uniformed officer restrained Keith. Ethan held Andre back.

"Come on, bro," Parnell whispered to Keith. "You know this isn't helping anything."

"It's his punk ass fault that this Mackenzie and her daughter have been abducted and Joel is dead," Keith said.

Ethan hoped that he didn't hear Keith correctly. "What did you just say? What happened to Joel?"

Keith turned to Ethan. "Who are you?"

"I'm Andre's attorney and Joel's boyfriend. What's happening here, detective?"

"Thanks to your so-called client, Mackenzie and her daughter have both been abducted, and your boy had his throat cut open by a killer. He is in critical condition at Grady Hospital. They said it's not looking good."

Keith's words might as well have been a wrecking ball to Ethan's face.

———

He guided Mackenzie inside of Mrs. Russell's house, sitting her down on a wooden chair in the dining room. He took care not to be too rough with her, even if he already knew her fate. Mackenzie sobbed, her face still covered with the greasy towel. He almost felt sorry for her. As much as one could feel sorry for drowning a litter of stray kittens. It had to be done. His hatred of Andre Lang was that strong.

He unwrapped the towel from Mackenzie's head. It was too dark for her to see anything. She could only smell mothballs, mixed with hints of vanilla. He clicked on a bright light. Mackenzie's eyes slowly adjusted. The first thing that she saw was an arrangement of colorful plastic flowers in the center of a circular wood table. A curio cabinet in front of her showcased porcelain animals and ornate china. It reminded Mackenzie of her grandmother's old house in Savannah.

"Where is my daughter?" Mackenzie demanded, meeting her abductor' eyes.

He sat in the chair across from her.

"How about a little patients and gratitude?"

Mackenzie lunged at him. If her hands were not tied she would have clawed his eyes out.

"Where the fuck is my daughter."

"Tsk, Tsk," he waged his finger. "How can such a pretty lady have such a nasty mouth? Keep it up and you will never see her again."

Mackenzie concealed her rage for the moment. "Please."

"That's better." He glanced behind him "Bring her up," he yelled.

After a minute, a door creaked opened. Traci was pushed into the room. Her hands were tied and her eyes puffy from crying.

"Mom, what's happening?"

"Don't worry, Sweet T. I'm getting you out here."

"You really think so?" The person behind Traci came into the room. "'Cause, I don't."

Mackenzie couldn't believe who she saw. "Paula?"

CHAPTER 25

While Andre parked the car, Ethan barged through the automated sliding doors of the hospital emergency room. He was greeted by a symphony of coughs and moans from people in the waiting area who were there before him. Their emergencies were no less dire to them. He did not care. Finding out about Joel was his priority.

He rushed up to the reception desk, cutting off a woman who was complaining about her long wait time.

"Excuse me, ma'am," Ethan said, pushing past the woman.

The portly receptionist behind the plexiglass shot him a steely glare. "Sir, you need to wait your turn like everybody else," she said.

"I'm sorry. I'm looking for my friend. Joel Sanders. The ambulance just brought him here with serious injuries."

The receptionist, worn-out from long nights of working double shifts, had no sympathy to offer Ethan. She pointed at the other people in the waiting room. "You see all these people? Everybody in it has to wait their turn."

Before Ethan could respond, Andre came up behind him. He knew how insensitive the staff could be from his time working at Grady. Luckily, they seemed to have taken a liking to him.

"Hello, Shelia. How are you?" Her ice wall melted when she saw Andre.

"Hey, Dr. Lang," she blushed, batting her eyes. "How have you been? We miss you around here."

"I miss you guys too," Andre said. "Shelia can you help me and my friend out? We are looking for a friend of ours, Joel Sanders."

Shelia typed on her keyboard. "He is in surgery right now."

"Do you know his status?"

"I'm sorry, it's not updated yet. Dr. Adams is the ER surgeon-on-call. The only thing you can do is wait."

Mackenzie's eyes hot-lasered Paula. This was not the same mousy church girl, she had met who worked for Andre. Gone were the ultra-conservative clothes and tight bun hairdo. In their place was a feral creature wearing a tacky purple velour tracksuit and lots of makeup. Her dull brown hair looped over her shoulders. Hate seeped from her dark brown eyes.

"Paula, why are you doing this?" Mackenzie demanded to know. "What did we ever do to you?"

Paula didn't respond. She only held on to Traci, her nails digging deeper into Traci's arm. Traci winced with pain and fear. Paula's accomplice spoke up.

"You ever hear of the term collateral damage?" he asked Mackenzie. Mackenzie had her eyes locked on Traci. He pounded his fist so hard on the table that the room shook. "I asked you a question, bitch."

"I know what that means," Mackenzie said her focus still on Traci.

"Right 'cause you're a smart girl. A journalist, right? It's a shame you were stupid enough to get caught up with that fucker, Andre Lang. You were never part of the plan, but you are some handy collateral damage." He gestured for Paula to take Traci back to the basement.

"Nooo." Traci trembled. "Mom." Paula slapped a large swatch of duct tape across Traci's mouth before dragging her away.

Mackenzie tried to reason with him. "Please. I'll do whatever you want. Money. If it's money you want, I will empty out all my bank accounts. Whatever you want. Just let my daughter go."

He scoffed, shaking his head. "I don't want your money. I want Lang to suffer. No amount of money can buy that," he hissed in her ear, his hot breath reeking of stale cigarettes. He pulled out a flip cell phone and slammed it on the table. "You're going to call Lang and tell him that you are waiting for him at granny's house." Mackenzie looked up confused. He grabbed her by the neck and jerked her head. Mackenzie squeezed her eyes shut "I said call him, bitch. Lang will know what you mean. Tell him to come alone or there will be more blood on his hands."

———

Ethan sat quietly with Andre, drowning out the commotion of the ER waiting room. Joel was still in surgery and no one had come out yet to give any updates on his condition. The anxiety of not knowing had arrived long ago and stayed with Ethan, wrapping itself around his body, squeezing knots out of his head. He had not known Joel very long, but they were getting very close. There was something special about Joel—he could make a person laugh even when they tried hard to stay mad. The fierce loyalty he had for his friends was inspiring. Joel didn't deserve to die this way.

Andre's phone rang. It was an unknown number. "Hello."

He heard a muffled voice sobbing. "Andre, I need you to meet me at your granny's house. Come alone." The line went dead.

"Mackenzie?" Andre said as he stood.

Ethan looked up at him. "What's going on?"

"I'm texting you Keith's number," he said, heading for the exit. Tell him to get to my house ASAP."

———————

By the time Keith had arrived back at the precinct, his phone had rung nonstop. None of the calls were encouraging news. He leaned back in his desk chair, staring at the ceiling as if he were watching a suspenseful movie: In it, almost fifteen hours had passed since the crisis began. There were still no credible hits on the Amber alert. Time on a digital clock was clicking down to catastrophe. The hero was running out options to save the day.

Keith ran his hand over his face, mulling over the things he felt he should have done better and his perceived failures: Maybe if he hadn't acted like such an asshole toward Joel when they first met, Mackenzie would have never met Andre and she would not be in this situation. It was stupid of him not to warn her immediately when he first found out about Andre's past.

Parnell leaned in office doorway for an update. Keith's face contorted in frustration was obvious, but he asked anyway.

"Any word, man?"

Keith didn't take his eyes off the ceiling.

"No. This is either a repeat or a copycat of what happened to Lang's family in Memphis. That didn't turn out good." Keith's cell phone rang. "Wilson," he answered.

"Keith this is Ethan. You need to get to Andre's place ASAP."

———————

Amusement glistened in his eyes as he stared at Mackenzie, trying to make eye contact with her. She wouldn't give him the satisfaction. Such a shame. He felt the urge to see her face. She was not the first beautiful woman that he had killed, nor would she be his last. Like the others, she was just a tool of vengeance for what was taken from him. He lit a cigarette and blew a perfect smoke ring in her face. She coughed but did not budge, refusing to play his game, no matter what.

"I bet you're wondering, why this is happening to you? What did you possibly do to deserve this? All you wanted was to be in love," he said. Mackenzie continued her stony concentration on the floor. "No need for you to answer. I know your husband died of cancer a few years back. After that, you tried your best to build a new life for you and your children. Believe it or not, I can actually admire that. Too bad you fell for a sorry piece-of-shit who doesn't deserve any of it. See, you don't know that baby killer like I do." He ran his calloused hand along Mackenzie's left cheek. "Tell you what, I'll do you a favor and give you some real cock before Lang gets here." He chuckled at his offer. "Your daughter can join us, too. I heard she loves to fuck."

Mackenzie's head snapped up. She glared at him, disgusted by the enjoyment of his shallow, grey eyes. Dried blood trailing from his buzz cut to his forehead added to her nausea. Her fury boiled hotter than an erupting volcano over what he was doing to her family. To

Joel. To Nate. There was no way she would let this monster touch her child. She would die before she let that happen.

"OK. Come closer, sexy," she said, smiling and cocking her head in the flirty way that she knew turned men on. "It can just be you and me."

He leaned into her. "That's my pretty girl."

Mackenzie lunged at him. "Motherfucker if you go anywhere near my child, I'll kill you," she shouted. "I will fucking kill you."

He pulled back, laughing heartlessly at how he had riled her. "Whoa. Look at you Miss Feisty. We're going to have a whole lot of fun."

Paula came running into the room. "What's going on?"

"Nothing." He dismissed her. "Just letting our guest here know how things are going to be. Go back down to the basement." Paula didn't move. She was fixated on Mackenzie. "I said go back in the fucking basement, bitch."

"Don't get distracted by this slut. Remember our plan. You promised me."

There was a knock at the front door. He smiled at Mackenzie.

"Looks like the guest of honor has arrived." In rapid giddy motions, he wrapped the towel back around Mackenzie's head and shoved her into Paula's arms. He peeped through the peak hole. "Dr. Andre-fuckin'-Lang," he said, opening the door, his eyebrows raised with excitement. "Come on in. Let's chat."

———

Andre cautiously entered the house, sweeping the room that he had been in many times before visiting Mrs. Russell. Mackenzie, Traci or even Mrs. Russell were nowhere in sight. A long sharp hunting knife was placed ominously in the center of the dining room table, prepared to cut through its victim with minimum pressure.

"What is this? Where is Mackenzie and Traci?"

"Do you know who I am?" He sat at a dining room chair and propped up his dirty boots on the table. He picked up the knife to scrape the palm of hands, grinning wider than a Cheshire cat enjoying the cat and mouse game that he was playing.

Andre did not recognize the smug asshole sitting in front of him. He appeared to be in his early thirties. His tongue dripped with a definitive Cajun accent. His hair was shaved like a skinhead's, emphasizing a square forehead and a patchy beard sprouting from his pasty face. A large colorful tattoo of dragon was etched on his sinewy bare chest. There were many secrets teased in his shallow, grey eyes that he would no doubt delight in exposing.

"I'm not fucking playing games with you. Where the fuck is Mackenzie, Traci, and Mrs. Russell?"

He chuckled, waving off Andre's anger. "You're so pathetic. Don't worry about your bitch and her brat. They're safe…for now. Had to get rid of the nosey old bitch, though. Have a seat. I would offer you a beer, but granny only has cranberry juice in the frig." He offered his hand for Andre to shake. "Name's Sebastian Bordeaux. It's time you learn the truth about, Rene."

Andre slapped away the outreached hand. As much as it triggered him hearing this person speak about Rene as if he knew her. Saving Mackenzie and Traci was his only mission.

"Where is Mackenzie and her daughter?"

"That was rude. I told you that they're safe. Have a seat." He pointed at the chair next to him. "I won't ask again." His eerily calm voice signified serious consequences if Andre didn't comply.

Andre reluctantly sat down. "Where are they?"

He let out a hard breath. "I see we are not going to get down to real business until you know about those two bitches. Paula," he shouted. "Bring the mama back bitch up here."

After a moment, Paula appeared, leading Mackenzie into the room. Mackenzie's wrists were tightly secured with zip ties and her mouth gagged with duct tape. Paula shoved her down on the couch with a loud thud. Andre could see the fear in her eyes. He stood to help her.

Sebastian slammed his fist on the table. "Sit the fuck down. This ain't no petting zoo."

Andre sat back down. "Paula, what are the hell are you doing?"

Paula pointed at her accomplice. "Helping Sebastian deliver justice to a baby killer," she said.

"That she is," Sebastian said pleased with the look of utter betrayal on Andre's face. "I couldn't have done it without her."

"Ethan Carlson." Ethan lifted his head, hearing his name being called. "Ethan Carlson." He raised his hand and stood to meet Dr. Adams. He was wearing characteristic blue scrubs. A serious look on his brown face didn't signify that he was coming out to deliver good news.

Ethan cleared his voice. "Yes," he said. "I'm Ethan."

"Are you waiting for Mr. Joel Sanders?"

"Yes, how is he?"

"Well, he lost a lot of blood. He's still in critical condition, but we have him stable right now."

Ethan breathed a cautious sigh of relief. "Can I see him?"

"He's not awake, but sure. Follow me."

Dr. Adams led Ethan down a hallway that lacked as much personality as the rest of the hospital. The floors were slate grey and the walls a shade of faded dove. Patients laid out on stretchers lining either sides of the walls seemed to have been forgotten. When they had finally reached Joel's room the doctor showed Ethan through the door before leaving.

Ethan paused at the sight of Joel laying in the bed. There were so many bandages wrapped around his neck and torso that he appeared to be a mummy. A tube was coming out of his mouth to assist his breathing. The weak steady blip of a heart monitor did not look encouraging. Ethan went over to the bed.

"Damn, Joel," he whispered. "What have they done to you?"

———————

Andre could not believe the scene playing in front of him—Paula giving an Oscar worthy performance as the shy, devoted friend who turns out to be working with the killer. Anger and confusion bubbled in his chest.

"I asked you a question, Paula," Andre said again. "What the hell are you doing?"

Paula moved over to massage Sebastian's shoulders, her expression matching the smugness on his face. "What can I say? The dick is powerful," she shrugged, bending over to kiss him. She pointed at Andre. "So is our desire to punish you for your sins."

"Is Chris in on this, too?" Andre asked.

Paula chuckled and shook her head. "Poor gullible doctor. Chris was never in on it. He was just somebody we hired to fuck with you. Didn't you notice the subtle ways he mentioned your family every time he saw you?" She kissed Sebastian on the forehead. "It was obvious."

"Go take her back, baby," Sebastian instructed Paula, smacking her ass. Paula yanked Mackenzie away. He turned his attention to Andre. "Satisfied?"

"Where is Traci and Mrs. Russell?"

He sighed hard, shaking his head in frustration. "You still don't get it. Still think that this is a game. Traci is in the basement, but I told you already that I killed the old bitch, just like I killed Dana and your sissy friend."

"Why are you and doing this?"

"Because of you. Because of Rene."

"What the hell does Rene have to do with any of this?"

He grinned and was happy to connect the dots of Andre's confusion. "Ding, ding, ding. There's the million-dollar question ladies and gentlemen. He win's a prize," he said, clapping like a game show host amping up an imaginary audience. He switched back to seriousness. "You ignored Rene. Didn't give a shit about her needs."

"That's a lie. I loved Rene."

He banged the butt of the knife on the table. "Shut the fuck up and listen. That's the problem. Your selfish ass never listened to her, not even enough to realize that she was slipping away. Too busy killing babies to notice that she had fallen in love with another man. You didn't know her. When did you ever participate in any of the activism that she was passionate about? No protesting the killing of little black kids by cops or even fighting for the environment. Rene loved that kind of shit." He paused before continuing his rant. "You didn't even want to go to North Carolina with her to visit her family for Thanksgiving. How selfish is that? You just believed this fantasy that she was happy so long as she was living in that big house and driving a German car. But she wasn't happy at all. I first met her when she was my professor at U of M. She was a lonely woman in need of attention, and I gave it to her. At first it was just phone calls and text. Then we would meet up every chance we got to just talk about anything—life, the state of the world, how many stars there are in the fucking sky. Anything. We couldn't deny the electricity between us. She set up a group trip to go protest at Standing Rock. That's where we first made love. When she first decided to leave your pathetic ass for me."

Andre's face dropped remembering the time Rene went to North Dakota to protest. One of many times that he was uninterested. *This can't be real.*

"You're lying," he said.

"Believe what you want. Just know that she loved me." He gripped his crouch. "And this big white cock deep inside of her, especially in your bed, on your high-priced sheets while you were out killing babies. When we found out that she was pregnant she didn't know if the kid was yours or mine." He stood and kicked over the chair next to him. "She aborted him without telling me because she decided to stay with you for the sake of Zhuri." He slapped his chest hard, his voice cracking, liquid pain leaking from his eyes. "That was my baby. I loved Rene, but she had to die. You suffering for not appreciating her was killing two birds with one stone."

Andre's head was spinning hearing that the life he knew was a lie. That he was the cause, including Rene aborting a child that might have been his.

"What about Zhuri? What did she have to do with this?"

"They say hurt people hurt people. If my baby had to die, your little bitch had to die, too. The sad thing is that all that's happening now was supposed to be just about you. But then you had to go fall in love again with a bitch that has a pretty daughter. Trying to recreate your family. Pathetic. That was just too good to pass up and Paula was all too happy to help." He pointed the knife at Andre's face. "Now, you're going to suffer even more when you watch them die, too. If you beg, I might just put you out of your misery."

CHAPTER 26

Mackenzie huddled next to Traci on the dank basement floor. The entire room reeked off death. Traci was crying and shivering like she had been dropped in subzero water. All around them were boxes full of what must have been several decades of Mrs. Thomas' hoarding. Paula stood at the top of the stairs listening to the heated arguing coming from the living room. She looked back at Mackenzie.

"It's going down," she said with glee in her eyes. "You know that you're about to die, right? So is your baby killing boyfriend." She pranced down the stairs over to Traci's. "Aww. Don't cry, pretty, little green eyes," she said, twirling Traci's hair. "Since you love fornicating so much we might take our time with you. You would like that wouldn't you?" She let out a wicked cackle before she went back up to the door.

Mackenzie had to do something. Giving up on saving her child was not an option. She franticly scanned the basement until she spotted a small, blacked out window in the corner. She would have to break free from her restraints and get pass Paula to get to it. It was now or never. She searched her mind, remembering doing research for a story on how to escape if you were ever tied up. Her wrist seared with pain from the zip ties. Mackenzie stood and raised her hands above her head. She swung them down and outwards to try to tear the ties apart. It didn't work. She tried again, this time her hands broke free. Paula came charging down the stairs.

"What the hell do you think you're doing? We're not done with you," she shouted.

She shoved Mackenzie, sending her stumbling over the boxes of junk crowding the basement floor. Mackenzie managed to keep herself from falling. Instinctively, she grabbed a heavy brass curtain rod that was sticking out of a box. Morphing into a championship slugger, Mackenzie cracked the side of Paula's head like she was scoring the game winning home run. Paula dropped to the ground like a deflated baseball. Mackenzie kept hitting her until she was sure Paula had stopped moving. She ran over to the window. It was nailed shut so she used the rod to break the glass. She rushed back over to Traci.

"We're getting out of here."

———

Andre had heard enough. Adrenalin pumping through his veins, he sized Sebastian up for the best way to take him down. His slight frame didn't look like much of a threat, but the knife he wielded as an extension of his hand could be problematic.

The loud sound of glass shattering came from the direction of basement.

Sebastian jerked toward the noise taking his eyes off Andre for a second. Andre made his move. Calling on his amateur boxing skills, he punched Sebastian in the jaw and chin just as his head turned back around. Sebastian spun sideways, still clutching the deadly knife. He slashed Andre across the center of his chest and deeper than a carved turkey along his right forearm. Andre jumped back feeling the flesh tear free from his arm, the pain searing white hot.

"Time to die." Sebastian said with murder in his eyes. Andre used his good arm to try to wrestle the knife from his hand. Sebastian head-butted him in the nose. Blood erupting across his face, he swept Andre's legs from underneath him, slamming his back against the floor. Sebastian stomped him repeatedly in the head and chest, his heavy boots leaving bloody footprints on Andre's shirt. "She killed my baby 'cause of you. She had to die 'cause of you."

Andre felt his consciousness fading. He maneuvered to kick Sebastian's kneecap almost hard enough to break it. Sebastian fell backwards, sending the knife skidding across the floor. Andre pushed himself back on his feet with one arm, ignoring the pain from every part of his body. He moved as fast as he could to get to the knife before Sebastian could. Sebastian wobbled up on his right leg, ready to continue their death match. He saw Andre holding the knife and gasping to catch his breath.

"What the fuck you gonna do with that? You're too much of a pussy to even keep your family alive."

Andre blacked out. "This, motherfucker." He charged at Sebastian, plunging the knife deep into his chest, twisting it until it found the exact spot for deadly impact. Sebastian dropped to the ground, blood spewing from him like a fountain. Andre kneeled over him, stabbing his body again and again. "Die!" he demanded, his voice quivering.

In a blue unmarked police Taurus, Keith raced to Andre's house. He feared what he would find when he got there. All he had gotten from the Ethan's ominous phone call was that he needed to get there ASAP. Parnell was in the passenger seat. Backup SWAT officers crackled over the radio that they were in proximity to the location. Keith lay on the horn and flashed his lights several times behind a truck that was blocking his path. He hit a speed bump so hard that it felt like the bottom of the car ripped off.

"Slow down a bro. The streets over here aren't set up for driving like this." Parnell said.

The truck pulled over to the side of the road. Keith zoomed around it, ignoring Parnell's warning. Mackenzie's life was in danger. His car screeched to a halt in front of Andre's grey craftsman with bone white trim. His Range Rover was parked in the front.

Keith jumped out. He gestured for Parnell to go around to the backyard.

With their guns drawn, Parnell snuck around back. Keith crept up on the front porch. He got down on his knees and cupped his face to the window. All the lights were off in the house. The only sound was from a dog yapping and scratching at the door.

Two backup cars stopped in front of the house. He whistled for Parnell and ran up to the officers. Sirens roared in the distance from other units responding to the call.

"What's the situation?" one of SWAT officers asked. He looked extra prepared in tactical gear and a vest.

Keith, like Parnell, only had on sweat shirts and jeans.

"A mother and her daughter were abducted. Got a tip that their being held at this location." Keith paused as he thought of Joel. He prayed that this would not turn into another homicide. "Suspect is armed and dangerous, so we need to control the situation before we go in." The officer nodded and gathered his team to advise them before they prepared to storm Andre's house.

———————

Mackenzie held on tightly to Traci's hand as they ran through the backyard. It was dark, so she could not make out where they were. She could only see silhouettes of trees and bushes between the nondescript houses. A streetlight guided her toward a beacon of hope. There were several police cars parked in the middle of the street. Traci was still so paralyzed by fear that she could not run. Mackenzie stopped, tossed Traci's arm around her shoulders and held her up.

"Come on, baby. You can do it. We have to get out of here."

"OK, mom. I'm sorry."

"Don't be, baby," she said, breathing raggedly. She summoned the strength for a final sprint to safety. "Help. We need help."

Keith heard Mackenzie's voice echoing in the dark. He shined a flashlight toward her cries and saw her stumbling toward them with Traci. He rushed toward her. Parnell and several officers followed. Parnell lifted Traci in his arms. Keith let Mackenzie lean on him as he led her toward his car. "I got you Mackenzie."

"The killer still has Andre in the house," she whispered.

———————

The ICU room erupted with loud alarm warnings. Ethan was sitting next to Joel's bed. He jerked out of his lucid dreaming, not sure if what he was hearing was real.

Doctor Adams and two nurses rushed into the room. He quickly accessed the monitors. "He's hemorrhaging." Doctor Adams said.

"We need to get him into surgery ASAP." He turned to and an RN. "Call to get an OR room ready."

"Yes, doctor." The nurse walked quickly toward Ethan who was standing next to the door.

"Is he going to be OK?" Ethan asked her.

"Sir, you need to please leave so we can our job." She pushed Ethan out the room. He stood at the door, watching through the window. Two orderlies blew past him. The blips of the heart monitor were replaced with a piercing wail.

"Shit. He's coding." Doctor Adams turned to the other nurse. "No time to move him. Prep the defibrillator."

"Clear." the nurse yelled. Doctor Adams placed the defibrillator paddles on Joel's chest. His body jolted with fifteen hundred volts of electricity running through him. No response.

"Again," Doctor Adams ordered.

Again, Joel's body convulsed. The heart monitor continued its threat, indicating no response from the patient.

"Again."

"Clear."

Joel's body jolted with energy from the lifesaving current for the third time.

Serval squad cars blocked the front of Mrs. Russell house. A few of neighbors began to gather on the sidewalk to see what all the commotion was about. Officers cautioned them to stay back for their safety. Keith was kneeling at the passenger door of his car talking to Mackenzie. Traci was buckled in the back slumped against the door, a blanket wrapped around her shoulders to warm her up. The cuts on their arms and hands didn't appear to be too serious, but Keith had insisted that they go to the hospital to get treated for the shock of what they had just been through.

"Everything is going to be OK," Keith assured Mackenzie, patting her thigh.

She only nodded her head, tight lipped and distant. He closed the car door and walked around to the driver side window where Parnell was sitting.

"You guys about to going in?" Parnell asked.

Keith glanced over his shoulder at the SWAT officers. They were gathered in the front, ready to execute their instructions.

"Yeah, man. Lang is still in there."

A SWAT officer walked over carrying a vest. He handed it to Keith. "Figured you could use this," he said. "We're ready to go in as soon as you are."

Keith nodded then he turned back to Parnell.

"Take care of them for me. Keep me posted. We will get statements later."

"Be safe," Parnell said, driving off.

Keith put on the vest. "Let's go," he said to the SWAT officer.

Three officers went around to the back of the house. Keith and two more went up on the front porch. One of the officers used a battering ram to bust open the door. Keith carefully went in before him. He quickly accessed the gory scene. The house was trashed from an obvious fight. Andre was on the floor kneeled next to a bloody body. Keith pointed his gun at him.

"Drop the knife, Andre."

Andre was in a daze. It took a second for him to process the command being shouted at him.

"I said drop the knife."

Andre snapped out of his trance and threw the knife on the floor. He stood up with his hands raised.

"Mackenzie and Traci are in the basement," he said, franticly. "Help them."

"We already got them," Keith said, lowering his gun. "They're safe." He radioed to the rest of the SWAT to come in. They swarmed the entire house. A few minutes later, Paula was brought up from the basement in handcuffs. Her faced was bruised and bloody but she still managed to snicker "baby killer" to Andre as they shuffled her out the door.

Mackenzie and Traci were in a trauma room at Grady Hospital. Parnell was able to use his police credentials to get them immediate assistance. On the way over to the hospital, neither of them had wanted to talk about what they had just been through. Silence and the chance to breathe a little easier was what they both needed. A nurse came back into their room. She informed Mackenzie that both of their vitals were normal. The cuts on their hand and arms had only required cleaning and bandages. Mackenzie's arm that had required four stitches. She told Mackenzie that they were free to leave as soon as she filled out some paper work. Mackenzie thanked her for her help.

Mackenzie sat next to Traci. She was still shaken up, but more alert than she had been. Mackenzie dreaded what finding out that Joel was dead would do to her.

"How are you feeling, baby?"

"I'm OK," Traci whispered.

Mackenzie looked at Traci trying to put on a brave front. She teared-up as she squeezed her child tightly and kissed her forehead. "I'll be right back. Let me sign this paperwork so we can go home.."

"OK."

Mackenzie went across the hall to the nurse's station. She used their phone to find out Nate's status and let him know that she and Traci would be home soon. Just as she was hanging up, she saw Ethan walking toward her. She ran up to him and threw her arms around his neck.

"What are you still doing here," Mackenzie asked.

"Joel just got out surgery."

Mackenzie was confused. The last time that she saw Joel he was surely dead.

"What do you mean?"

"We were close to losing him, but he is alive." Ethan was happy to report that news.

Mackenzie didn't know what to say. She hugged Ethan again.

"Where is he?" she asked, wiping her face.

"Follow me."

Ethan led Mackenzie to Joel's room. He was in the bed with a tube coming out of his mouth. Thick bandages were wrapped around his neck, but his eyes were open. His face lit up when he saw her.

She went over to the bed. "You scared me," she said. She leaned over to kiss his forehead. He struggled to speak but could only mumble sounds. Mackenzie knew that he was trying to ask about Traci. "Traci is safe, too. She is in the room down the hall."

Joel squeezed Mackenzie's hand. Silent tears of relief tears welled in his eyes.

———

Immediately after he had given his statement to the police, Andre called and texted Mackenzie several times to check on her and Traci. She didn't reply until the next day, but she told him that her and her family were doing as well as could be expected. He had asked if it was OK for him to stop by her house to talk. She agreed that there was much that they needed to discuss. He had found out from Ethan that Joel had survived. For that, he was relived. Still, his insides burned knowing that his life had led to so much death and betrayal. His mind and soul could not reconcile any of it.

He pulled into Mackenzie's driveway. He sat in the car for a moment then up went to ring the bell. Mackenzie opened the door; barefoot, wearing black leggings, and a grey CAU sweatshirt. He wanted to reach out and hold her but that didn't seem appropriate.

"Hey," she said with her voice raspy. He followed her to the living room. She sat Indian style on the couch and he sat next to her.

"How are you, Mackenzie? How is Traci, Nate and Joel?"

"Traci is up in her room hanging with her friend, Antonio. She is still shaken up, but I will make sure that she gets all the help that she needs to completely recover. Nate was fortunate to just have a flesh wound. Joel is still in the ICU. His doctors are optimistic about his recovery." She paused. "How are you, Andre?"

He was not sure how to answer. Physically he was fine, but mentally and emotionally he had sunk deep into quicksand. He didn't see a way for him to escape this time.

"I'm OK," he said. "Been better."

She pointed at the large knot above his right eye and the makeshift wrap around his arm that was seeping blood. "I can tell. Did you go to the hospital?"

He glanced at his arm like it didn't matter. "I deserve this for not being honest and putting you and your family in a horrible situation."

"No, you don't, Andre. I thought about it. Yes, I was angry with you for not telling me the truth, but you just wanted a fresh start. You didn't know all this craziness was going to happen." She looked at his arm again. "Let me get some gauze and peroxide to clean and wrap that arm better before it gets infected." She started to get up. He guided her back down to the sofa.

"Don't worry about me, Mackenzie." he said, looking into her eyes. He stroked her cheek. "You're such an amazing and forgiving person. The way you care about everybody. How devoted you are to your children. All that you have overcome. It was so easy for me to fall in love with you and envision a future with you and your kids. I know we could have been happy together if circumstances were different. If I were different." He slowly shook his head. "But I'm not. What I've learned over the past day destroyed me. The life that I thought I knew was a lie. The woman who I thought was happy with me was not. She was killed because of me." He started to tear up and his words were trembling. "My child was killed because of me. I don't know how I can recover from knowing this truth." He could no longer keep the tears from flowing down his face.

"It wouldn't be fair of me to dump all of my baggage on you. It's best to conquer these demons on my own. I will always have a special place for you in my heart, but right now it's too filled with darkness for me to love anybody."

Mackenzie moved over to hug him tightly. They cried together before she spoke. When she lifted his chin the pain that she saw in his eyes was indescribable.

"I can't even begin to imagine what you're going through. Finding out the truth about your wife cut deep, but you have to let go of the past so that you can heal. So, you can move forward. Continuing to punish yourself is no way to live, and you deserve so much better." She hugged him again. "I wish you well, Andre. No regrets."

EPILOGUE

One Year Later

Delta flight 4587 parked at gate S7 in the E Concourse of Atlanta's Hatfield-Jackson International Airport. The cabin lights blinked on followed by a ding, announcing that it was OK for the passengers to disembark. They say whatever happened in Vegas, stayed in Vegas, but Mackenzie and Keith would have a story to tell: bad shows, laughing until their stomachs hurt, partying, drinking, and gambling for the thrill of losing money. Mackenzie was glad that she had gone with Keith. The weekend getaway was what they both needed. They retrieved their bags from the overhead compartment, then shuffled down the narrow aisle, back to reality.

Mackenzie had pulled back from working as much so that she could focus on raising her children. It wasn't always easy, but Nate and Beverly were still there to help when she needed them.

With a lot of therapy, Traci was getting back to normal. She had accepted into early admission programs at Cornell and Princeton, but decided to attend her father's alma mater, Emory U. She wanted to remain close to home.

Antonio was headed to UCLA on a full basketball scholarship to work his way to the NBA. If he didn't get drafted, he would have no problem moving back to Atlanta to pursue a career in sports medicine.

Joel was doing much better. He was finally opening his own design firm and things were off to a good start. He continued physical therapy sessions but had Ethan by his side. The two of them had gotten engaged and planned a wedding for the following spring.

Following his heart, Keith had quit working for the APD, and had put his passport to good use traveling the world. Mackenzie was looking forward to joining him in Kenya for his next trip. Back in Atlanta, he had co-founded a non-profit organization for at-risk kids to reach them before the streets killed their hopes and dreams. Mackenzie had seen a change for the better in him. The easy persona that he was famous for was back. They didn't have any expectations on their relationship, but it was good to hang out with him from time to time.

They got off the plane and boarded the crammed train to baggage claim. When they reached the top of the escalator, Keith went to use the men's room. Mackenzie waited at the carousel for their luggage to appear. As she was texting Nate, she looked up and caught a glimpse of Andre hurrying through the terminal. He didn't see her, but he was wearing a grey suit and carrying a briefcase. Wherever he was going, it was probably work related.

She didn't speak to him often outside of the occasional phone call or text, but he had told her that he was back in therapy full-time. He had moved to Chicago and working as a medical director for a city free clinic. She knew that it was not easy for him. Mackenzie was glad that he was trying hard to pick up the pieces of his life. Even though the time that they had spent together was brief, being with

Andre taught her that it was OK to open her heart to love again. She hoped that she had done the same for him.

CPSIA information can be obtained
at www.ICGtesting.com
Printed in the USA
BVHW03s1942200618
519562BV00001B/47/P